D0270673

WHAT WAS NEVER SAID

WHAT
WAS
NEVER
SAID

EMMA CRAIGIE

Published by
Short Books, Unit 316, ScreenWorks, 22 Highbury Grove, N5 2ER

10 9 8 7 6 5 4 3 2 1

Copyright © Emma Craigie 2015

Emma Craigie has asserted her right under the Copyright,
Designs and Patents Act 1988 to be identified as the
author of this work. All rights reserved. No part of this publication
may be reproduced, stored in a retrieval system or transmitted in any
form, or by any means (electronic, mechanical, or otherwise) without
the prior written permission of both the copyright owners
and the publisher.

A CIP catalogue record for this book
is available from the British Library.

ISBN: 978-1-78072-1-798

Printed and bound by CPI Group (UK) Ltd, Croydon, CR0 4YY

Every effort has been made to trace the copyright holder and to
obtain their permission for the use of copyright material in this book.
The publisher apologises for any error or omission in this regard and
would be grateful if notified of any credits or corrections that should
be incorporated in future reprints or editions of this book.

This book is dedicated to the inspirational students of Integrate Bristol and the City Academy Bristol.

your old anthem burns a hole in stomach
i am the daughter of immigrants
my home is a home of longing
i am swollen with language i cannot afford to forget
i am homesick for a home i have never lived in
last night i dreamt of you
your warm mouth on the soles of my feet
you were humid
your palms flat on my bare shoulders
you carried me home
my mothers village
my fathers first kiss
dear god,
was this what belonging felt like
my god,
i'd never wanted anything so bad.

dear Mogadishu, warsan shire

I

THE CUTTER CAME LAST NIGHT. I recognised her: her black clothes, her narrow face and the yellow whites of her eyes.

The first time I met her, I was five years old. The summer before we came to England.

Mum had scrubbed us and dressed us in our best clothes. We were prancing around the courtyard when we heard the drummers, and the sounds of the women singing and the stamp of their dancing. The three of us ran out to join them, holding hands, and I was happy because I was in the middle of the big girls. You, Rahma on one side and your friend Yasmin on the other.

There was a crowd of women. Their scarves and dresses ballooned as they swayed. Yellow. Red. Pink. Blue. Green. All the beautiful colours. We stopped just short of them.

I have been through this so many times in my head. They were clapping their hands. They made space for us in the circle and we joined in the dance.

I can see the dust we scuffed up; Yasmin's hair bouncing as she kicked her legs high and skipped to the

11

words of the songs. I can see the blue of your dress, Rahma, as it floated around you. I can see the shine of your eyes and your big new teeth which looked too large for your mouth and stuck out when you laughed.

We were hot and sweaty when Yasmin's mother came over and whispered something to Yasmin. She took her by the hand and led her away. I was afraid we were in trouble, but Yasmin looked back over her shoulder and smiled. I kicked the dust and stamped my hardest. We sang at the top of our voices, warbling like little birds, as high and loud as we could.

I have often tried to imagine what could have happened if we had stopped singing then and listened. Would we have heard her? Could we have stopped it?

We heard nothing but the singing and the drumming and then Mum came and took your hand.

"Wait here," she told me, her breath in my ear. "I will come back for you in a minute." I couldn't wait. I was dancing faster and faster and longing for it to be my turn.

So I was on my own when I heard the screaming. The voices of the singers dipped and I heard your voice, Rahma, piercing the air, flying above my head.

I broke away.

I broke away and the further I got from the singers, the easier it was to hear that the screams were coming from our house. Grandma was standing in the doorway.

"Go back!" she hissed at me, twisting her hands, "Go back to the dancing!"

I could still hear you, Rahma; I could hear you,

though your screams were getting quieter, spreading and fading.

"What's happened?" I thought there must have been an accident.

"None of your business. Go back!" Grandma glared at me, jutting her jaw towards the dancers. Her stuck-out tooth biting down on her lower lip, "Go!"

I ran back a short distance and crouched down to watch the house. I could hear the rhythm of the drums, the wails of the singing. There was no more screaming. I shrank into the narrow shade of a date tree, my back squashed against its rough prickly trunk. Slowly the shade spread in front of me until I could stretch out my legs. A woman came out of our doorway. I had never seen her before. She was all in black, like a poor woman. She spoke to Grandma, something long and difficult. Her hands chopped the air. I couldn't hear what she was saying.

Then Grandma went inside. I took my chance and ran for it, trying to reach the doorway before Grandma came back out.

The woman in black was walking away, but she heard me. She stopped and waited. She stretched out her thin hand and grabbed my arm. She squeezed it tightly and fixed me with her marble eyes.

"Are you the sister?" Her voice was croaky.

I nodded. I was staring at the ground; her black dress was streaked with brown dust around the bottom. I glanced up quickly to see if I could see whether she had long ears under her head scarf. Mum always told us

13

stories about the long-eared witch who would catch us and eat us if we were naughty.

"You will have to wait now until next year." She leant down towards me, her sick sweet breath on my face. I stopped breathing, I closed my eyes and suddenly she let go.

I ran to the house. I don't know what I was expecting. As I went through the door, I was hit by the smell of frankincense. You, Rahma, were lying on our mattress, with a blood stained sheet across your legs. Your eyes were open but you didn't look at me. Mum was wiping your forehead with a cloth; she didn't look at me either. Two ladies I didn't know, fat ladies, were squatting down, scrubbing at a great dark stain on the floor. It made no sense.

Mum looked up. Her hair had fallen out of her scarf. "Out!" she yelled. "Mother, get Zahra out of here!"

Grandma picked me up from under the arms and carried me out.

It was evening when they let me in. I held your hand, Rahma. I stroked your hand and gave you all the love I had to give you. I hope you know that.

It was a long time before I understood what had happened.

I watched Mum and Grandma wash you and wrap you in cloths. I watched Dad lift you. Your heavy head and your long legs hung down on either side of his outstretched arms. I was not allowed to go with you.

The house was full of women. The sweat and colour of the dancers. They were quieter now, murmuring.

After you'd gone, after Dad had taken you away,

Mum crouched down and covered her face with her hands. I stood behind her and stroked her back as she rocked on her heels.

That night Yasmin's mother took me home with her and fed me dates and rice and goat's meat. The left-overs from the celebration. She gave me water, and held the cup as if I were a baby. Then she put me down to sleep beside Yasmin.

Yasmin was groaning. I didn't recognise the shadows of the room.

2

I **DON'T KNOW** why Somalis love the snow, but most of us who fled the civil war have been drawn to somewhere cold. Minnesota, for example, is our most popular destination in the US. If you search on the Internet for the climate in Minnesota you will see a picture from 1881 of a train stuck in snow drifts which tower above it. There are many more Somalis in the cold northern European countries than the warm south. Lots of us are in freezing Canada. And even in Australia, we have gravitated to a region called Victoria, famed for its snow ski slopes.

Of course there is very little snow in Somalia. Dad always told us that if we climbed to the top of the highest mountain in the country we would see it. I've realised since that he was exaggerating. It only occasionally snows on the top of Mount Shimbiri. Certainly on the day that they photographed there for Google Earth there was no snow at all - only dark trees and swirly slopes making amazing patterns – like psychedelic flowers or marbled fingers – but no frost. I've zoomed right in on the palest bits which could almost be white at a distance, but they look pretty sandy up close.

When we arrived in England I thought it was snowing. I followed Mum out on to the airplane steps and felt this freezing raw wetness on my face like little knives jabbing my face. That first feeling of England hollowed me out. We didn't know what cold was. It can carve right through you and skin your bones.

At night in Mogadishu we used to lie on our mattress and listen to the grown-ups talking. I never understood what they were saying, but you would explain the strange words to me: America, Europe, passport, dollars. These were the words that we used when we made our city of twigs and stones in the yard. If one of us needed to pee, and didn't want to spoil the game, we'd say, "Give me my passport. I need to go to America to fetch some dollars." Or, if you were bored and wanted to stop playing, and perhaps go and see what Yasmin and Jimcaale were up to, you'd say, "Snow! Snow! Everyone indoors!" and that would signal the end of the game and you would wave your fingers in the air and send down an invisible snowfall. We were fascinated by snow. The idea that refreshing flakes of cool soft ice could fall from the sky seemed impossibly exciting. We imagined ourselves in a snow storm, faces tilted upwards, tongues sticking out. But we also knew it could be deadly. Yas told us that her dad's uncle had died walking home in the snow in Minnesota. He got dazed by the whiteness and died of cold.

Recently on YouTube I watched a film about a woman who escaped the war in Somalia and ended up in America. Ohio. She had never been cold before. She didn't know what it was. Her teeth were chattering and her body was shivering and she thought she was going to die. In fact, she nearly did die. She ended up in intensive care with severe dehydration. She didn't know what it felt like to be thirsty without being hot. She didn't realise that humans always need to drink. They put her on drips and gave her blankets and she was fine.

It wasn't snowing, but sleeting when we got off the plane. I had never heard of sleet. There'd never been any sleet in our yard city. I stepped out of the plane and this icy wet wind came at me and whipped at my skirts. I thought the stewardess should have warned us. Just a moment beforehand, she'd given me her big lipstick smile, and wished me 'a good onward journey' as her eyes passed on to the person behind me, and she didn't say a thing like: 'Watch out! You're about to be sliced in two by an ice blast!'

I've sort of got used to the cold climate here. I've got a warm coat and thick tights and furry boots for the winter. But it's now, when the weather's meant to be warmer, that it bothers me the most. I hate the grey skies. And even more I hate the weak sun which shines so pale and ducks behind clouds and can't even drum up the energy to warm the air. I hate the disappointment of a sunny day. I long for the dark blue sky of Africa and the pounding warmth.

3

WHEN I FIRST woke up that next morning, I thought I was snuggled up with you, Rahma, as usual. But even before I opened my eyes, I realised the light was wrong. It was blue, shining through a cloth in the window. Then I remembered the dancing, and stroking your hand, and your body in Dad's arms.

Yasmin was looking at me. Lying flat. Her hair was all matted; her face screwed thin. The corners of her lips were cracked and sore.

"Tell Mum that I need to pee." Even her voice had shrunk.

"What?"

"I can't move. Look – " She tried to push down the sheet covering her. She couldn't reach very far. I lifted it. Her long thin legs were tied together at the ankles. We were lying on dried blood.

"What happened?"

She shook her head. "It hurts. I can't…"

Her eyes were leaking tears. I ran fast.

Aunty Noor was in the yard leaning over a small fire, cooking breakfast. Her back to me.

"Aunty Noor," she wasn't really my aunt, it was just out of politeness, "Aunty Noor, Yasmin needs you quickly."

Jimcaale was crouched by the fire, waiting for a pancake. Immediately he uncoiled and leapt up.

"Come back," Aunty Noor shouted. She lifted the pan off the fire. "It's not you she needs. Stay here."

He dropped back down and poked a twig into the flames. Then he looked at me and stretched his lips sideways into a smile that was also a frown.

"You know the lady in black?" I said.

He nodded.

"Is she the long-eared witch?"

He laughed and shook his head. "Don't be stupid!"

Then he held out a closed fist and let five little stones fall to the ground.

"Do you know how to play?" he asked. "You can go first."

4

MUM HASN'T WARNED us that they're coming. She never tells us anything. We get in from school and the kitchen is full of the smell of smoke and burnt meat. Mum's standing over a pan frying chicken, flattening it with a wooden spatula, pressing it into the sizzling oil. The worktop's covered with cling-filmed dishes – salad, rice, little meat pies. Samsam drops her bag and runs straight over to start picking.

"Hands off! You girls need to go and change out of your uniforms. I've put your best clothes on your beds for you. Be quick now. We are having visitors. From Somalia. My cousins' cousins. You've met them, Zahra, but you were probably too young to remember."

As we run upstairs, she shouts after us: "You can do your homework in the morning!"

We're still upstairs when the doorbell rings. Sam's in her knickers, waving her scarf in the air and dancing round the bedroom like Lady Gaga. She's six now. She was born here, in the living-room, not long after we moved in. Before we had a sofa or even a carpet. You should have heard Mum yell. Maybe

21

you did, when I was born.

The doorbell rings and I look out of the bedroom window and see a line of women coming up the garden path. Sam's scrambling into her dress, flinging her scarf around her head.

I'm halfway down the stairs when I realise. I stop dead. I stick out an arm to stop Samsam running past me. She's standing there, thin as a cane, all in black like before, staring at us with her marble eyes, leaning on the pull-out handle of a small black suitcase.

"Zahra!" Mum's behind her, holding open the front door. Beyond her there are two more women: fat ladies in bright pink and orange gowns and behind them I can see Aunty Noor, tall and upright. "Zahra! Come and welcome our guests."

It's like a film. I can see what's going on right now but I can't change it. I carry on down the stairs, taking Samsam's hand.

The woman in black lets go of her bag and moves towards me. She squeezes my arm with her skeletal fingers. I remember the feeling. "How you have grown," she says quietly. She bends down to Samsam, "Hello, little girl."

Her words are cut off by a cough. She straightens up and twists her mouth to the side, lifting her scarf to cover her face. Her eyes fill with water. Her cough is rough and low and it goes on and on. The fat ladies are packed into the hall behind her. Aunty Noor is in the doorway. "Zahra," says Mum, "Get a glass of water. Samsam, take our guests into the living-room."

I go through to the kitchen and turn the tap on full

blast and I hold my hands under it as it runs cold. I wonder what's in the suitcase. Knives? Razors? Rope? Herbs?

I fill up a jug and put it on a tray with some glasses. In the sitting-room the fat ladies are whooping over Samsam. I put the tray down the coffee table and pour the cutter a glass of water. She has stopped coughing. She is standing by the window looking out at the street. Her bag is at her feet. She nods and lifts the glass to her mouth. She takes tiny sips.

The orange lady grabs my shoulders. She swivels me round and looks me in the eyes and chuckles with laughter. She squashes me into her huge soft bosom, pushing my nose into a mist of frankincense and sweat.

"Hello girls, hello girls! Goodness me, Fadumo! What fine daughters you have! Noor was telling us how beautiful they are but really, I never imagined! You will have to take good care of these two!"

She drops down, giggling, and the two of them stuff themselves into the sofa, rearranging their scarves.

"What a nice house. Haven't you done well! What lovely girls! Ha ha ha!" Aunty Noor offers the cutter Dad's armchair and then perches beside her.

"Zahra," says Mum. "Offer our guests tea or coffee."

"Tea or coffee?" I say, flatly. Mum glares at me.

"I'm fine," says the cutter.

"Are we talking Somali tea, or English?" asks pink lady.

I hesitate.

"She can make either, can't you, Zahra. Which

would you prefer?"

"I'd love a nice cup of Somali tea."

"Me too," says the orange lady, beaming brightly.

"Can you make me a coffee?" Aunty Noor smiles. It's not a real question so I don't answer.

"Just an English tea for me," says Mum.

"Two Somali teas, one English tea, one coffee," I repeat.

"How well brought up your daughters are!" The pink lady burbles. "And so grown up! Mind you, never too late! Did you make these outfits? They're so beautiful. Come here, darling. Let me feel the fabric." She stretches out a hand and rubs her fingers on Samsam's dress.

"Come and give me a hand, Sam," I say. She's doing a little twirl. "Come on. I need your help in the kitchen."

5

I LOVE THE SOUND of the language of Somali. It is a whole-mouthed language. It bubbles like spring water on the tongue, but then there's a pause and the sound is flung to the back of the throat. It growls. It calls up pain from the deep. It is the language of the desert. The language of nomads. The language of sailors and traders. It is a language which moves across the mouth as its people move across the world. A whole-mouthed language of a brave people.

I love the sound of English. It is easy, light fluid. Tip of the tongue. Hand up, busy and keen. It can rise into the nose, straight through to the brain. It is good for thinking in. It is the language of promise and future, a language which is easy to pick up, but you cannot howl in it. It will never go that low.

6

LAST SEPTEMBER Yasmin started at uni in London. When she came home for the Christmas holidays, Aunty Noor arranged a get-together. It was a really miserable evening: freezing cold rain blown into our faces by a sideways wind. We walked up the street carrying tubs of salad and a huge cheesecake under a plastic dome. We arrived in a wet flap and Yasmin opened the door.

My first thought was that she looked incredibly beautiful. She was framed by the doorway and wearing a huge headscarf like a crown on her head. That was fine. It was what she was wearing below that set Mum off: a big tartan shirt and skinny jeans.

"Oh my days, Yasmin!" Mum shouted, as soon as she saw her, before we were even in the dry, "What is this? I can't believe it. What is this?"

Yasmin stepped back to let us in and we stood dripping in the hallway as Mum carried on: "Why are you naked? Goodness me, Noor!" She yelled through to the kitchen, "What has London done to your girl? Why are you allowing this?" Then back to Yasmin. "What's going on? Have you lost your morals and your religion?

I suppose you are trying to look cool to fit in with your university friends."

"Hey, Aunty. Nice to see you too!" Yas flashed her a smile.

"I can't believe it!" Mum marched into the kitchen, and Samsam and I followed, carrying the food. Dad, who had been hanging behind us, keeping quiet, slipped into the living-room where the men were watching the football.

"How can you allow this, Noor? Where's the discipline? Have you lost control of your daughter?"

Aunty Noor was standing with her back to us chopping furiously. She didn't turn around; she spoke slowly, deliberately: "This is what comes from a British education. We encourage them, we support them and this is what we get for it."

"Anyone want some crisps?" Yas asked, her voice bright and hard. "I'll get the bowl from the living-room before the men finish them." She swung out of the room, pulling the door sharply behind her.

Samsam looked at me and then followed after her.

"Put the salads in bowls" Mum told me. "And take the lid off the cheesecake. It can stay on that plate. What else needs doing, Noor?"

"We are pretty much ready," Noor sighed. "The girls can take everything through."

Yas, reappeared, holding a big bowl with some crisp crumbs in the bottom.

"Why do you want it all in the living-room? Isn't it easier if everyone helps themselves in here?"

Noor untied her apron. "If we have it in the living-room the men can easily help themselves to seconds."

"Oh sorry of course. We've got to make sure the men are happy. Can't have them making any effort to feed themselves." She put the empty crisp bowl on top of the cheesecake lid, picked up a tower of plates and walked out.

"Oh my my!" said Mum. "What is she studying at that university?"

"Law," said Noor quietly, and rubbed a hand across her face. "At least she'll be able to support herself. More than I can say for her brother at this rate."

I grabbed a pile of napkins and followed Yas out.

The living-room was packed: Uncle Hasan, Jim-caale, our dad and a couple of friends of Uncle Hasan, Mukhtar and Ahmed, fellow taxi drivers who are always there; I don't think they've got families of their own. None of them looked up as we went in, but there was a collective gasp. Nothing to do with the array of food we were setting out: someone had hit the post.

Jim pressed pause, and stood up.

"Oh Noor!" Mum boomed, "Look at the size of him! What have you been feeding him? You must be taller than your father now! When did I last see you? It's not that long!"

Jim gave me a what-is-she-like look. "Is there any more to bring through?"

"Oh Fadumo," said Aunty Noor, ignoring him and distributing serving spoons amongst the dishes. "You haven't heard our latest drama. Jim, tell them what happened last night."

Jim raised his eyebrows and stuck a serving spoon

28

into a big pot of curry.

Aunty Noor leaned towards Mum and whispered loudly, "He was stopped by the police."

"What?!" Mum screeched. I don't know why she couldn't see that he didn't want a big song and dance about it. "Why?" she added, more precisely.

He shrugged his new wide shoulders, "I just crossed the road in the wrong place." He took his plate and went back to sit in front of the TV.

"What do you mean you just crossed the road in the wrong place? That's not a criminal offence!"

"They were coming out of the cinema. Ten at night. Two police officers appear from nowhere and tell them they have to cross at the lights." Aunty Noor started ladling out the curry.

"We weren't coming out of the cinema. We'd been bowling." Jim said through a mouthful of food. He pressed play.

"Anyway. It was down by the multiplex. Where they've got these new lights?"

"The lights have been there for years." Jim kept his eyes on the TV.

Aunty Noor lowered her voice, "They'll pick these boys up for anything. You can't trust them. Take this to your father, Zahra." She handed me a heaped plate of rice and curry.

"This country!" Mum muttered, tonging salad on top of Dad's plate.

"You can't trust the police anywhere in the world," said Ahmed. He had hauled himself out of the sofa and was gawping at the food. He rubbed his belly and smiled at the table. He had a shiny patch on the front of his beige jumper from all that rubbing.

"You should complain," said Mum to Aunty Noor.

Aunty Noor snorted, "You must be mad! What's that going to do?"

"Please!" said Uncle Hasan, "Can we get on with serving the food and get back to the football?"

"You can help yourselves," said Aunty Noor.

Mukhtar unrolled his long legs and pushed himself up from the floor.

"Come on," said Yas. "Let's go to my room."

Mum and Samsam and Aunty Noor headed back to the kitchen. Yas and I carried our plates upstairs. She slammed her bedroom door behind us and moved a pile of books and a suitcase on to her bed to make some space on the floor for us to sit down.

"I've really had enough," she said, stabbing an innocent piece of carrot. "I don't know how you stand it. I've got one more day and then I'm back to London for New Years. If it all gets too much, just give me a call and come and stay."

She put down her plate and leant over and put on some music. Someone Tempest rapping fast and furiously. She slammed up the volume and I felt I'd missed the moment. We listened to the Tempest woman's problems instead. I've never talked to Yas about what happened. And now it's so long ago it never seems like the right time to bring it up. I've never told anybody. I can't talk to Mum. She wells up if ever your name is mentioned, Rahma. Sometimes I wonder if I've imagined the whole thing.

7

THE FAT LADIES are squealing with excitement. "Oh Fadumo. What a spread! Aren't you spoiling us!"

Back to the kitchen for plates, napkins, spoons. I'm on automatic. We're outnumbered. I fill a metal bowl with warm water and carry it through; Sam follows with a clean towel. The water sloshes alarmingly from edge to edge. The ladies haul themselves out of the sofa and plunge their hands into the basin in turn. They both shake their wrists, spraying water like dogs, before taking the towel from Sam.

They load their plates with food, and lower themselves carefully to sit. The cutter takes a meat pie and nibbles it slowly. Aunty Noor is full of chat. Their journey. The weather in England. What kind of a summer it might be.

Sam is gobbling cheerfully. She's sitting on the floor just beside the cutter's chair. My stomach has closed. I put a few bits on my plate. I'm trying to think fast. I don't know what to do, where to go. I need to speak to Yas.

They're talking about the war. The Youth. The

31

camps. I wish Yas was closer. I can't think how we could get to London. If we go to any of my Somali friends their mothers will definitely take my Mum's side, and send us straight home.

I'm prodding a little heap of damp green leaves on my plate, hoping no one notices that I'm not eating. Mum's voice sounds artificial. High-pitched. She looks at the guests, she looks at her plate, but she doesn't even glance in my direction.

"How were things when you left?"

The lady in the orange launches into a rapid fire answer, pausing now and then to sweep up a piece of fried chicken and tear off a mouthful with her teeth, at which point the pink lady takes over, naming names I didn't know, places I can't picture.

Every now and then, the ladies glance at each other and one of them gives Mum a hard look, or raises one eyebrow, which I take to mean, there is more I could say here, if you understand me, but not in front of these girls. I get the gist of what they're saying though: things have been terrible but now they are a bit better. I think of the bombed streets, the bullet-marked walls, the hollow windows, the stripped trees, the lighthouse.

"What about the militants?"

The cutter coughs again.

"Well, there are stories. Bad, bad stories. The Youth is very big. But the political situation has definitely improved. Some of the armies are being disbanded…" She stops and looks across to the cutter who's now bent over with coughing.

"Samsam, pass her her water," says Mum.

The cutter takes a sip.

"Thank you," she says.

She puts down the glass and stands up slowly. She puts her hand out and rests it briefly on Samsam's head, "Can you show me where the bathroom is?"

"I will." I jump up. "It's upstairs."

8

GRANDMA WALKED me back home later that morning. She held my hand tight, crushing my little finger. I didn't say anything. I had to do a skip every few steps to keep up with her; she was walking fast, pulling my arm out of its socket. She didn't say anything, until we reached our house and she opened the door and shouted:

"She's here."

Mum was sitting with your blue dress on her lap. She lifted me up and sat me on top of it. She held me tight against her shoulder. Her arms around my arms.

I inhaled her. I wanted to stay there forever.

9

I WAIT on the upstairs landing and then follow the cutter back downstairs.

"What happens to the soldiers of the disbanded armies?" Aunty Noor is asking, putting her coffee cup down onto the carpet.

"Well – they try to find work. But it's hard for them," the pink lady has specks of mayonnaise around her lips. "They wander around." She pauses. "It is good you got out when you did." Again, she raises an eyebrow, "I'm afraid it is no longer a safe place for girls to grow up."

Mum starts boasting about how well we're doing at school.

"Samsam has reached level 2. It's a very good level. And Zahra now, she is taking GCSEs in ten subjects."

"Eight," I say. "Excuse me."

I push myself up off the carpet.

"You will be wanting to find them good husbands." The fat ladies giggle.

"Would anyone like some more water?" I ask. I pick up the jug. I'm hoping to fill all the glasses and slip out to the kitchen to refill it.

"I'm fine, thank you," says Aunty Noor; no one else replies. I put down the jug and slip out anyway.

From the other side of the door I can hear the voice of the cutter, "It is high time, Fadumo."

I don't wait to hear what it's high time for. I dash upstairs. I grab my handbag. Throw my phone in it. Check my purse – I have £15. Then I go in the bathroom and dial Yas. I flush the toilet, to cover my voice, as it answers, but I know it's going to be a machine and it is. I text her "Please call" and then put it on vibrate and slip it into the front of my bra. I hurry downstairs and go straight into the kitchen. I put my handbag down by the back door and pick up a dish of meat pies that somehow got left on the side.

"Oh," says Mum, as I put them down in the living-room, "I'm not sure we're going to need those." Her voice is still unnaturally high, "Would anyone like a little pie? Or maybe some potato salad?"

The lady in pink takes both and the rest of us sit politely waiting for her to eat up. It's like torture. I'm watching her fork and I'm still not sure of my plan. I can feel a vibration in my bra but I can't dash off again immediately. She's talking about her son who works for some kind of telephone business in Nairobi. Making lots of money. She keeps lifting bits of potato into the air, and then, before the fork reaches her mouth, she lowers it back to her plate and throws her head back and laughs, or she bursts out with some irrelevant detail about the house he's building: the colour of the marble worktops, the style of the taps. Finally, she's finished. I give it one more polite moment and then I

36

say, "Hey Sam, let's clear the dishes."

Mum beams at me. Which makes me feel bad.

We take the first load through to the kitchen. I whisk the phone out of my bra. It's just a message from O2. I pop it back.

"Why don't you run a sink of hot soapy water and we can start the washing up? I'll get the rest of the dishes."

Samsam looks at me as if I'm mad, "We don't have to do it now, do we? Can't we wait till they've gone?"

"Well it would be nice to help Mum," I lie.

I go back to the living-room.

"There is rice pudding on the cooker, Zahra. You'll need to tip it into a serving bowl and we'll want some little plates and spoons."

Dessert? I hadn't thought of dessert.

I go back to the kitchen. "Apparently we've got dessert, Sam. Don't worry about the washing up, we can do that later. Can you carry some bowls through?"

I spoon the pale grey pudding into a yellow dish and follow her through. Mum dollops it out and the pink lady wobbles with excitement, "Oh, what a treat! It's not every day we get dessert! You are spoiling us!"

Sam and I sit back down on the living-room floor and suck the sweet rice off our spoons. The cutter isn't eating pudding. She stands up and crosses over to the window. She bends down and unzips a front pocket on her suitcase.

"Would anyone like some more tea?" I jump up.

Mum looks a bit surprised that I'm being so thoughtful, but she covers it well. "That would be lovely."

The cutter brings out a white handkerchief and

37

coughs gently into it.

"Come on, Sam," I say. "Come and give me a hand."

"I haven't finished my rice pudding."

"Bring it with you."

We go through to the kitchen and I put on the kettle and set the taps running.

"Sam," I say, "Mum wants to talk to the visitors in private. She says we can go to the park."

"What about the tea?"

"We'll make it when we get back."

She starts jumping up and down. She loves the park.

"Stay still," I want to seem normal, but I'm whispering. I velcro her shoes, slip on my pumps, pick up my bag, and out we go. Very gently, I pull the back door to. Along the path, past the gardens, no running, nothing that would draw attention. Out on to the street. I'm praying none of our neighbours see us and luckily nobody's out in their garden.

"Hey Sam, hold my hand." She slips her small, soft fingers into mine and starts skipping along the road. All the time I've got my eye out for neighbours. If we get seen then Mum will be able to find out which direction we've gone in, as soon as she realises we've scarpered, which could be already.

We get to the end of our road fine. We turn into Chaucer Street and at the far end I can see a woman from the mosque who Mum is quite friendly with. She's fiddling with her key in her front door.

"Hang on," I murmur to Sam. "Hang on," I repeat, thinking desperately what to say, "I've got a stone in my shoe."

I take off one shoe and make as if to tip something out. Luckily Sam's absorbed in her own toe-to-toe, heel-to-heel little dance movements. The woman's front door is closing behind her. The rest of the street is quiet. At last, we come to the end of the road and cross straight over to the park. There's hardly ever any Somalis in the park. I let go of Samsam.

10

"'WHO CAN I HEAR running away? Whose little foot-steps can I hear?'

"'No one, mother.'

"'Oh yes I can, I can hear the sound of children running. They may be many miles away but you can be sure that I will be able to catch them. Stoke up the fire and fill the big pot with water. It needs to be boiling by the time I come back.'"

The fire flared. I could see the long-eared witch's hut in the blackened twigs. I could see the flames of her fire. I leant into Mum as her voice softened.

"And as they ran the children promised God that they would always be good. For the long-eared witch can run as fast as the wind but she can never catch a child who is good."

I closed my eyes and screwed my whole body into a wanting-to-be-goodness. Then I looked across to you, Rahma, to see if you were doing the same, because I couldn't bear it if the witch caught you. But you didn't look like you were even listening to the story. You were leaning backwards and staring up at the stars. The stars scared me. I slid down and put my head on Mum's lap.

"So the good children reached home safe and sound and the long-eared witch went to bed hungry."

II

Up close, it's a very flat dull red. There are two pots holding identical plants either side of it. This is mad. I don't even like Annie. I don't know her family. But I can't think of anyone else.

Annie pointed out her house back in the Easter holidays. Mum had been hoovering and Sam had been hyper. She was playing a game of getting round the living-room without touching the floor. She made a balletic leap from the sofa to Dad's chair but unfortunately knocked over a photo frame on the mantelpiece as she flew past. It was a picture of Grandma, sitting outside her house in Mogadishu. I've no idea who took it and gave it to her, or how it survived the bomb, but somehow Mum had kept it safe all the way to England. The frame hit the brick fire surround and the glass broke. Unlucky. It so nearly landed on the carpet. Mum went mad. I thought she was going to hit Sam with the hoover tube but she managed to restrain herself. She shook it furiously and told me to get Sam out of the house.

Luckily it wasn't raining. The sky was grey. Dull,

browny grey and damp but not actually tipping it down.

We went to the supermarket first – Mum wanted us to get some onions. I held Sam's hand across the car park and over the road. Then I let go and she set off across the grass. By the time I got to the playground she was on the very top of the wooden castle.

There was nobody about. I went round the back of castle mound, where they've got a couple of benches. I sat down – only a bit wet – and checked my phone. I looked up and there were two girls from school heading for the swings. They hadn't seen me. Annie Prest from my art class – such a show-off – and Krysty Something who's in English. I think she's Polish.

Krysty pulled a packet of cigarettes from her pocket and they both took one. Annie seemed to have a lighter. They sat down on the kids' swings and that's when they noticed me. Annie gave me a big wave.

"Fancy a fag?" she yelled.

I shook my head. "No thanks." My voice cracked slightly.

Annie bounced off the swing and headed towards me.

"What d'ya say?"

"Nothing. Just, no thanks."

"It's the end of the packet. I was only joking. I can't see you smoking. What you doing here?" She plonked herself beside me. Her eyes were too bright. The other girl kicked up her heels and leant back to swing, holding her cigarette in her lips.

"I brought my sister to play." I could see Sam shooting down the castle slide towards us.

Annie pulled her parka under her bottom and crossed her long legging-clad legs.

"Look what I've just got," she said, and lifted up her top to show me her scrawny tummy. There was a silver dolphin hovering over her belly button, and a little metal ball poking through the skin above. "This morning. Up Union St. You know?"

I didn't. It was gross. Her belly was see-through white, veiny. I didn't know what to say. She laughed, "Have you got any piercings? You could have all sorts of things hidden under that outfit!"

"No."

"You should. Look, Krysty's got her tongue done. Come here, Krysty." She yelled, "Stick it out!"

Krysty slipped off the swing and came over with her tongue sticking out. It looked thick, swollen. She sat down beside Annie, took a puff on her cigarette and pulled out her phone.

"What about tattoos? Got any secret tattoos?"

I wasn't finding this as funny as Annie was, "No."

Samsam had tumbled off the end of the slide and was walking towards us.

"I'm thinking of getting a Leo sign on my shoulder."

"Right."

"What's a Leo sign?" Sam asked her and slipped onto my lap.

"Um, it's a kind of a squiggle, an upside down U. You know, the star sign Leo."

Samsam frowned, "Zah, will you come on the climbing frame with me?"

"Sure."

44

"I'll come too!" said Annie and stamped out her cigarette on the woodchip ground.

Krysty exhaled a long stream of smoke and carried on texting. We climbed the mound and up to the top of the climbing frame. It's not very high but you can see the whole park, the road around it and the houses beyond. The bright stripes of the supermarket.

"That's where I live," said Annie. "The one with the red front door." She hooked her knees over a bar and hung down, her thin pale hair straggling limply. From upside down she obviously saw what I saw because she immediately raised her body and jumped down. "Gotta go. See ya."

Two guys had joined Krysty. White guys. Dreadlocks. Bums on show and woolly hats. They didn't look round when Annie joined them but she soon got their attention by hoiking up her T-shirt, flashing her dolphin.

I would have offered to push Samsam on the swings, at least to get her started, but I didn't want to be over that side of the mound. The boys were handing something round. I was saved by spit: a definite enough drop of rain to make Sam agree to come home.

"Bye!" she called, but none of them heard her. I raced her down from the castle all the way to the park gates with the onions thumping against my thighs.

12

THE LONGER we're out on the streets, the sooner we'll be spotted. We've been in the park about quarter of an hour. Sam's been climbing and I've been trying to get through to Yas. It keeps going straight to answerphone. We're running out of time.

The door is opened by a very tall boy with his hair in a pony-tail. He stares at us in amazement.

"Is Annie in?"

"Sorry no." He puts his hand back on the latch as if he's about to close it, then he hesitates, "Do you want me to give her a message?"

I've told Sam that I need to borrow a book for homework. "Um, could we come in and wait for her?"

"Well…" His eyebrows shoot up, "To be honest I've no idea when she's going to be back. I'll see if Mum knows. Wait there a sec." He pushes the door shut.

We stand on the doorstep for what seems like forever. I'm keeping a look out. An old Asian man in a long white shirt walks slowly past, his arms stretched by plastic supermarket bags. A white woman comes in the opposite direction, dragging a screaming toddler along the pavement. Samsam's staring. My phone starts buzzing. I slip my hand under my scarf and pull it out the top of my dress. It's Mum. I'm surprised it took her this long. The door opens, and I drop the phone, unanswered, into my bag.

This time it's a woman, and she opens the door wide. She's got a puzzled smile and frizzy grey hair bursting out of a blue bandana.

"I'm sorry," she says. "I was in my studio. I can't hear a thing from there. Do come in."

She leads us into a huge kitchen. There's a square table covered with the debris of tea and toast: half empty mugs; butter which has been attacked in its packet; a pot of jam with a knife sticking out of it; a teapot and a bottle of milk; plates covered with black crumbs.

The tall boy is standing at the sink laughing. Two other boys stand up as we come in and the three of them hurry out the room, muttering hello, then thud upstairs. Perhaps it was stupid to come.

"Abe says you're looking for Annie? I'm afraid she's not here. Can I help?"

"Um, do you know when she's going to be back?"

"I'm not sure. Hang on, let me give her a ring. What are your names?"

We answer in turn. There's a sudden blast of loud music from upstairs, and then the volume goes down to an unidentifiable bass.

"Beautiful names. I'm Letitia. But everyone calls me Lettice. Now, where will I find a phone?"

She pats her trouser pockets and I notice that her

clothes are covered in dabs of different coloured paints.

She goes to the door to the hallway and shouts: "Abe! Have you seen a phone?" There's no reply. "I don't know where I've put my mobile," she adds pointlessly.

Sam extracts a telephone from a stack of magazines and newspapers on the seat of a sofa. "Is this it?"

"Oh brilliant. Yes, that'll do. Let's see…" She presses in the numbers and gives us a big smile as it rings. "Annie, hi love. I've got a girl called Zahra here with her little sister. Are you going to be back soon? Yes, I think so. OK, I'll tell her. That's fine. OK. We'll eat about 7.00. Well please try. OK. See you later."

She puts the phone down on top of a toaster.

"She's not going to be back for at least an hour. I could give you her number and you could text her. You've probably got it."

"OK. Thanks. Um. Would it be alright if we waited? It's a bit of a tricky thing. I'm not sure what to do."

"Is it something I can help with?"

"It's a book," says Sam, "she needs a book for homework and Annie's got it."

"Ah. OK. What's it called? We can go and have a look on her shelf."

"Um," I stare really hard into Lettice's eyes, trying to give her the hint that I want to say more than I'm saying. I say the words very slowly and deliberately, "Lettice, would you be able to help me look and perhaps my sister to could watch television or something, while you and I search for it?"

"But I'm the good finder!" Samsam tugs on my arm.

"You are indeed!" says Lettice. "And we might end

up having to get you to come and help us. But why don't we see what's on the telly. They often have good cartoons at this time of the day."

I could hug her.

She leads us through to a room the far side of the front door. The walls are covered with books and paintings. "Do you know how to turn it on? If not we can call Abe down."

"It's fine," says Sam, immediately spotting the remote on a bookshelf and pointing it towards the TV.

"You really have got a marvellous pair of eyes for finding things!" Lettice laughs. "I could do with you here all the time. I spend half my life looking for my phone or my glasses or something!"

We leave Sam flicking between channels and Lettice leads the way upstairs, "I'm afraid Annie's room is at the very top," she says. She stops on the first landing. "Was there something you wanted to tell me? If so, we can go and sit in my bedroom for a minute."

This is ridiculous. I don't know what I'm going to tell her. We should probably just go home. We go into her bedroom, which feels all wrong, and sit down on a little pink sofa by the window. They seem to have sofas in every room. Lettice smiles at me kindly, in this light I can see all the tiny lines radiating from her eyes.

"So," she says and pauses.

13

I HELD ONTO Dad's head. Tightly at first. My hands on his forehead, my legs over his shoulders, knocking against his chest. He held my ankles in his big warm hands. Every now and then he let go of one side and rested his hand briefly on your head, Rahma.

We walked right through the middle of the market without stopping. Through the strip of sun between the shade of the umbrellas on either side. I could see the tops of the umbrellas – white and striped and blue – and I could smell the food below: coffee, dates, oranges. We went past the turn-off to the fish market and I let go of Dad's head and clamped my hand over my nose and mouth. Up high like this the shouting of the stall holders, the blare of loud speakers and the distant sound of car horns seemed louder than ever. We went past Mum's favourite vegetable stall and turned off down a little street that was so narrow the stalls were only one side, the shady side, so there were no umbrellas, just tables of jumpers and pots and batteries all mixed together. We carried on along a series of these tiny streets until we reached the very end of the market. A row of men girl with four little packages of soap laid out on a dirty yellow cloth on the ground in front of her. She lifted one up for me to smell. There was a faint scent of something sweet and a strong stink of camel. She had a bowl of scummy water beside her and she was just lifting up a white cloth out of it to show me how clean it was when, suddenly, you pulled my arm.

"Dad's gone!"

I looked over to the row of men with their boxes. Dad wasn't there and nor was the man with the orange beard.

"Come on," you said, and grabbed my hand. I don't know how you knew your way back. You led me along streets I didn't recognise, pushing through the long skirts of fat women arguing over prices, past the men with the headscarves and the long guns, darting between sun and shade, the smells of meat and incense and rotting vegetables.

At last I saw something I knew: the two big plates of food painted on the wall of the restaurant at the end of our street. My armpit was aching. I don't think I'd ever walked so far in my life.

were sitting on white plastic chairs with their backs to a pink wall. In front of each of them was a large box, with a lid on, so you couldn't see what was inside.

Dad went up to a man on the end, an old man with a long orange beard who was sitting in front of a tall thin metal box. The next box along was square and wooden and painted red. I wished he had gone to that one.

Rahma, you wandered off to look at a goat and Dad popped me down so I could follow you. There was a

14

LETTICE IS GAZING at me with her pale grey eyes.

I swallow. "Um, I don't really need a book," I say. "I just said that to Sam because we needed to go somewhere and I didn't know what to tell her."

"You needed to go somewhere?"

She looks at me intently and I can feel a lump rising in my throat. "It was just Mum and Dad were having a big row." It's the first thing that comes into my head.

"Oh dear," she says. "We know all about that kind of thing here, I'm afraid."

I breathe through my teeth. "I thought it would be best to keep out of the way until things calmed down."

"Ok."

"Yep." I haven't thought this through.

"Does your Mum know where you are?" Her voice is really soft.

"Um, I said we were going to a friend's house." I lie.

From where I'm sitting I can see the park trees through her bedroom window. I wonder if Mum is out there, searching for us.

"I think you should ring your Mum and let her know

where you are. She'll be worried."

"Yes." I close my eyes. I can push the lump down. "Sure. I'll just check on Sam and then I'll give Mum a call."

Sam is engrossed in a cartoon, sitting right up close to the TV with her thumb in her mouth. I sit down on the sofa and call Yasmin. My fingers shake slightly as I press the screen.

I leave another message on her answerphone. As soon as I'm done, my phone starts vibrating. It's Mum again. I hold it until it stops, which is does just before Lettice comes in holding a tray. Apple juice, two glasses and a plate of chocolate chip cookies, a mug of tea.

"Did you manage to get hold of your Mum?"

"Um yeah."

Sam's still glued to the screen. Lettice persuades me to have some apple juice and I sit there sipping it, feeling awkward as she sits beside me and drinks her tea. We're both pretending to be interested in the telly.

My phone's vibrating again, but I ignore it.

"What did your Mum say?"

"Um. Well."

"Would you like to come and see my studio?"

I knock back the last bit of apple juice, "Sure."

"Samsam, if you need us just go through the kitchen and out into the garden. You'll see my little shed in front of you."

"OK," says Sam, "Can I have another biscuit?"

There's a little gravel path down the middle of the garden. Vegetables on one side, grass on the other.

"Hasn't it been a glorious day?" says Lettice, and opens her studio door.

Her little shed is actually quite big, but on the outside it looks like the kind of place where you might keep a spade and a lawn mower. It's half hidden by plants growing over it. There are no windows but the roof is made of glass, and one of the walls is basically a big wooden door.

Inside there are dozens of tiny paintings, hanging on the walls and propped on shelves. Mostly green and grey. I'm not sure what they're of – possibly the seaside on a bad day. Or maybe fields. Several of them have dark marks on them which could be posts or lonely figures. There are also piles and piles of pads of paper and pots of brushes and paints, bundles of pencils in jam jars, splayed like flowers. Lettice rests her bottom on the tall table which stands in the middle of the shed, high as my hips, a huge computer at one end and an open sketch pad at the other.

"So, what did your Mum say?"

"Well." For a moment I don't know what I'm going to say. And then the words just flow into my mouth. "Mum was in a bit of a state. She said Dad had been drinking. She thought it would be best if we didn't go back for a few hours. I was wondering, would it be OK if we stayed here?"

Her forehead crinkles. "Oh dear," she says, "I'm so sorry."

She goes so low on "so".

"Of course you can stay here. Would you like me to have a word with your Mum, so she knows you're safe?"

"Oh, that's alright. I explained."

"Are you sure? I can just have a quick word." She pulls her mobile out of her trouser pocket. I thought it was on the toaster.

"I don't think it would be a good moment, to be honest."

"Oh, really? OK." She puts her phone down on the table. "Are you doing Art?"

"Um. Yeah."

"Have you been doing this 'Disguise' project?"

"Um, kind of. I haven't really started yet."

"I was showing Annie this catalogue of an exhibition I went to a few years ago…" She stretches up to a high shelf and reaches for the edge of a big thin book, which is sticking out much further than the other books on the shelf. As she pulls it out, a couple of other books tumble and I bend down to pick them up off the floor. One of them has the most beautiful cover: it's made of a pale creamy grey cloth with soft mauve and green flowers which have been stitched on, and between the threads there are little flecks of gold paint.

"What's this? It's beautiful."

"Isn't it. It's just a pad of plain paper. I bought it in India – ooh, donkeys' years ago. I bought loads of them, because I loved them so much. You can have it."

"Really?"

"Yes, go on, take it. Everyone needs sketchpads. Look, this is what I wanted to show you. Frida Kahlo. Do her know her work?"

"Mum!"

Annie was coming up the gravel path across the

56

garden. "I hope you're not giving away my coursework secrets."

"No. Hi, love. I didn't think you were interested when I showed you."

Annie doesn't reply. She's chewing gum. She frowns as she looks at me. "Hi Zahra. Surprise visit. Is that your sister in the TV room?"

"Um, yeah. Is she in your way? We're going to be off shortly."

"Don't worry about it. I'm going up to my room. Krysty's here too. Catch you later. Give us a shout before you go."

"Sure." I put the pad in my bag. I don't know what I'm doing here. Maybe I've overreacted. I can feel my heart racing. Mum will be frantic with worry.

15

WE WERE WALKING along beside the empty beach. You, me and Mum. Two soldiers were sitting on the sand, their guns across their laps. Mum was looking out to sea. She kept saying, "Use your young eyes." She wanted to know if we could see Dad's fishing boat. You were shading your eyes with one hand and squinting, making out you were scanning the horizon. It was beginning to get dark and the sky and the sea were blurred. The only boats were at the far end of the beach, beside the old lighthouse. We were too far away to tell whether one of them was Dad's.

One of the soldiers stood up. He gestured with his gun, pointing us back in the direction we had just come from. Mum immediately turned for home and we followed behind her.

"That was a lucky escape," you whispered. "I thought we were going to have to go to the lighthouse. That's where the long-eared witch lives. Don't let her hear you." You tugged at your earlobe.

I looked over my shoulder. The lighthouse looked like a battered castle. A place where people had been killed. The windows were like dark eyes, watching us. I hurried on my tiptoes, as quietly as I could, silently promising and promising to be good.

16

ABE AND HIS friends are back in the kitchen. He is holding an empty tin in one hand and waving the lid in the air. "Who's eaten the biscuits?"

Krysty's sitting on the sofa, jutting out her jaw like Kiera Knightley and staring at her phone.

Annie sloshes boiling water on top of tea bags in a line of mugs and stirs them all vigorously, before dumping the teabags into a white jar labelled "compost". She adds milk along the line and back in a continuous movement.

"Hope you're going to clear that up!" Abe yells.

"You clear it up. I've made the tea." She hands me a mug.

"You going to come on up?" She says to me. "Krysty – you coming?"

"I'll just check Sam's OK."

"Fine, top floor when you're ready."

"OK." I feel so unsure what to do, I decide to just go with the flow.

"Come up – yeah – Krysty?" she repeats as she leaves the room.

Samsam is fine, only taking her thumb out of her mouth in order to laugh at the screen.

I decide to head up to the attic; Annie is plucking her eyebrows. She puts down her tweezers and faces me squarely.

"So – what's going on?" She's got lots of little red blotches around her eyes.

"There was a big row at home. I wasn't sure what to do. I came to see if you were in. Your Mum's been really kind. She says we can stay for a couple of hours but I don't want to be in your way. I'm not sure what to do really."

"Oh, stay. Stay. Don't worry about it. What happened?" She takes a big slurp of tea.

I'm not sure what to say. "Well, things are just difficult at the moment. It's hard to explain. I'm trying to get hold of my cousin Yasmin and work out what's the best thing to do."

"Where's your cousin Yasmin?"

"She's not actually a real cousin."

"OK. Where's your not-real cousin Yasmin?"

"London."

"Really? We're going there tomorrow. We could give you a lift. We're only going for the day, probably. Krysty's seeing this guy who lives up there and Nick – do you know Nick? – has offered to drive. I'm sure we can squeeze you into the car."

"Both of us?"

"I reckon. I'm sure there are five seats so why not..."

"Who's Nick?"

"Oh my God — he's this hot guy that used to be in

school. You'll know him by sight. Nick Butler. Do you remember he was one of that group that got excluded from sixth form last summer?"

I have no idea who she's talking about.

"Well, he's just passed his test and he's borrowing his dad's car. I'll text him now, just to double check."

"He's just passed his test?"

"Not just just. Weeks ago. At least a month. He's driven loads since then. He's a really good driver. He got a few minors but he reckons that's only because the examiner was biased against dreadlocks. You wouldn't believe the prejudice he gets. He's a really nice guy. You'll really like him."

I'm thinking that I'll have one more go at getting through to Yas, and if she doesn't answer, we'll go home. I don't want to end up in London with nowhere to go.

Annie jumps. "Come on, let's go and find Krysty."

Krysty is watching TV with Samsam. We squeeze on to the sofa beside them, but after about half a minute Annie has jumped up again and persuaded Krysty to go with her to see what the boys are up to.

I look at my phone and there's another missed call from home, but nothing from Yas. I decide to leave it another half hour before I try her again. I dig out the pad and flick through its empty pages. They're rough and bumpy, marked with tiny dark strands. I fish a pen out of my handbag and write five words.

17

UNCLE HASAN met us at Heathrow in his taxi. He brought Yas with him. Mum sat in the front and I sat in the back with Yas, eating satsumas and watching fat raindrops shudder on the window beside me. It was warm in the car. I wanted to stay there for ever. I couldn't see much through the rain and the misting windows but I had a sense of huge fast roads, juddering lorries, and some kind of greenness beyond. I must have fallen asleep because suddenly there were street lights, car lights, building lights and I realised we were in an enormous city.

"Welcome to Bristol!" said Yas.

18

LETTICE POPS HER HEAD round the door, "Any news from home?"

"Um, no."

"Well why don't you two stay for supper? You're really welcome to stay the night as well, so long as your Mum's OK with it."

"That's really kind. I'll give her another call."

"Great. Samsam, do you want to come and help me make some pesto?"

I text Yas again and stare at my phone, willing her to reply.

Dad is probably home now. Aunty Noor will have stayed. I imagine the ladies must have gone.

I suddenly realise that it's like the last time they left. That time Mum lost one daughter, now she'll be worrying that she's lost two.

Perhaps I'm wrong to think that they killed you, Rahma. Maybe it wasn't their fault. Everyone has a time to die. They could have done everything exactly right, but you still died.

I tap our home number into the phone. Mum would

never have invited them over if she thought they were to blame.

The thing that stops me pressing the green button is that I suddenly picture the suitcase. Why did she come with a suitcase? I imagine a small sharp knife wrapped in a towel. Or maybe a cloth. A gagging cloth.

It's like a scream of NO sets off in my stomach.

I click off the call, put my phone back in my bra and go through to the kitchen.

The room is full of the smell of garlic and basil. Sam is standing on a chair and tearing leaves into a food processor. Lettice is at the sink filling a big saucepan with water. I tell her Mum would be very grateful if we could stay the night. She takes the pan over to the cooker and shakes in some salt.

"Would it be good if I gave your mum a quick call now?"

"No, she's fine. Is there anything I can do?"

"How about chopping some tomatoes for a salad?"

She passes me a wooden board, and two plastic tubs of tomatoes. "Take a knife from that block thing." She unscrews the lid of a bottle of red wine, pours herself a glass and shows Sam how to switch on 'the whizzer'. The tomatoes are unexpectedly soft and ripe and difficult to slice. I have to use the tip of the blade to break the skin. It's a messy, juicy salad.

We eat supper in the garden. Abe's friends have gone. Lettice lights nightlights in jars and we put them along the middle of the table. Not that it's dark yet. Abe dishes out big bowls of green pasta.

I have been sat next to Abe. I suddenly feel shy. I don't want to be with these people. I busy myself with pepper and parmesan and scooping up tomatoes between two wooden serving spoons. Samsam is on my other side. She tucks right in.

Abe turns out to be full of chat. He clearly thinks I'm a spokesperson for Islam. A research opportunity. Why do some Muslim women cover their faces? Does anyone in my family? What do I think about it? I tell him I guess it's up to the individual. I tell him about going shopping with our neighbour who wears the veil, and how some randomer stopped their car and wound down the window in order to shout at her. I said "shout abuse". I didn't want to tell the whole table what he actually said, which was, "Get your fucking tits out, Missus."

"It makes me sick," he says. I'm not at all sure at first whether it's the veil or the abuse he objects to.

"This is supposed to be a liberal country. Why can't we live and let live? If a woman wants to put some black cloth across her face, let her get on with it."

"But what if the woman hasn't chosen to? What if someone has put her under pressure to wear the veil?" Annie shouts down from the other end of the table.

Lettice rubs her arms. It's getting cooler.

"A lot of women say they have chosen it." Abe shoots back. "We just don't respect what they're saying, because we don't agree with it."

"Well yeah, but they can be under pressure."

"We always think we know best in the west." Abe fills up his own wine glass and takes a big swig. "And frankly, it's bollocks."

"Abe," said Lettice quietly.

"Well it's true. We're so hypocritical…" He comes out with a great long list of stuff the British government does wrong, then he takes another glug of wine before hoovering up the pasta on his plate.

"Does anyone fancy pudding?" Lettice asks; she sounds tired. "I think there's some ice-cream in the freezer."

No one replies.

Sam leans her head against my arm. Heavy as concrete. Her eyelids are drooping.

"Can we go home now?" she whispers.

"Let's sort you out some bedding," says Lettice.

"We're having a sleep-over," I whisper to Samsam. Why didn't I tell her earlier? She looks puzzled.

"Annie," says Lettice, "do you want to get a sleeping bag for Samsam so Zahra can put her to bed in the sitting-room? And can you find a couple of towels for them? The rest of us can clear up."

Sam has a hand wash in the downstairs loo while I make her a nest on the floor with cushions. She won't take off her clothes. She wants her pyjamas. She wants Lion. She wants Mum.

"I don't want to be here!"

I explain that it's a treat. It's what big girls do. She glares at me.

"Hang on," I say. I dash off and wash my own hands, my feet as best I can. Then I go back and switch off the telly which she's just switched back on. I lay out the towels that Annie has given us and stand to face the back of the house which I reckon is eastish. I gesture for Samsam to come beside me, then I raise my hands. I don't want everyone to hear so I say the words quietly,

"*Allahu akbar*!" She follows beside me, murmuring the words, following my movements.

When we're done she's softer. I pull her dress over her head and unzip the sleeping bag. She wriggles in. I lie down behind her, on the edge of her nest of cushions, with my arms around her tummy. I quietly sing, "huuwa, huuwa" — like Mum does — until she falls asleep.

19

FOR THE FIRST few months we lived with Uncle Hasan and Aunty Noor. I shared a bed with Yas. I remember she had a pale pink duvet which we snuggled underneath and pretended we were in the clouds. We'd lie in bed all cosy and listen to the rain. Mum slept in Jimcaale's room and he slept on a mattress on the floor beside us which meant we couldn't open the bedroom door wide enough for grown-ups to come in.

Then Dad arrived and we got our own place, only four doors away. The same landlord, and the same layout and the same damp smell when you opened the cupboard doors in the kitchen. I thought all houses in England must be like this: a kitchen and a living-room downstairs and at the top of the stairs a tiny room with bubbly glass in the window so you couldn't see out, and a big bathtub with a shower in it. One big bedroom and two little. Brown carpet everywhere except the bathroom and kitchen where there were white tiles which felt like padded plastic and had whooshy marks all over them like spilt coffee.

I started school and I started wearing a headscarf. "You're a big girl now. It will keep you warm in this miserable weather." I'd never been so terrified. I couldn't understand what anyone was saying. Yas and Jim were in different classes. They taught me my first phrase in English. It was so hard to remember all the little sounds. I remember the teacher smiling when I first used it and I knew I'd got it wrong, "Please I go can toilet." I said it quietly so the other children wouldn't hear, but still they laughed.

At night I went back to my dreams of Mogadishu. I was in the street with you, Rahma. We knew there was a palace which was completely undamaged and we were trying to find it. We clambered over rubble, we crept along side streets. We never found it.

20

I GO THROUGH to the kitchen to ask Lettice where I can find another sleeping bag. She is sitting on the sofa looking at a tablet. She smiles at me and puts down her glass of wine.

"Is your sister OK?"

"Yes, she's just fallen asleep."

"Oh good. Do you think…" She stops at the sound of Annie and Krysty crashing down the stairs. They burst into the kitchen.

"Girls!" Her voice is surprisingly fierce. "Samsam's trying to sleep!"

"Oops, sorry!" says Annie and tiptoes exaggeratedly across the kitchen.

I ask about the sleeping bag.

"I've got one upstairs," says Annie. "Hang on a sec. I can dig it out for you. We're just going to heat something in the microwave. It's only going to take 10 seconds. Literally."

"You can't be hungry," says Lettice.

"WAX," mouths Annie. "Ooh, I tell a lie," she scrutinises the writing on the side of a little tub. "It's actually

71

15 seconds. Hope you don't mind waiting."

My bra vibrates and I pull the phone out from under my scarf.

It feels like the phone is making my heart race. I'm sure it's going to be Yasmin. But it's Mum again.

Lettice starts talking about bras not being good places to keep phones. Rays and cancer. Luckily the 15 seconds are up so I follow Annie and Krysty to the attic.

Annie whips off her leggings, "'Scuse me, Zahra, I hope you don't mind. I've got to do this while the wax is still hot. You'll find the sleeping bag in that chest at the bottom of the bed."

I find an orange sleeping bag on top of a pile of blankets.

"That's the one," she says, glancing at me over her shoulder. She's sat down on a towel on the floor in a tiny pair of pants with her legs spread open. "You might want a blanket as well."

"Thanks. This will be fine."

"Ay, ay ay! Fuck, this hurts. This is supposed to be the no-pain version. What the…?"

"There's no such thing as a no-pain version," says Krysty. She's staring hard at herself in a full-length mirror.

"Nick's fine to give you both a lift, by the way," says Annie. "He's aiming to get here around 11."

"Ok, we'll be ready." I reckon I can always pull out if I still haven't spoken to Yas. "Night, then. Sleep well."

"You too," Annie is bent over, examining her knicker area. She doesn't look up.

"Night," says Krysty, moving closer to the mirror. "I can't believe it, I have another spot coming. Have you got any Sudocrem?"

21

I GET DOWNSTAIRS and realise that I haven't got a toothbrush. The kitchen lights are off. There's toothpaste and a toothbrush in the downstairs loo but I don't want to use somebody's old toothbrush. I squirt a pea's worth of toothpaste on to my finger and rub it around my teeth. I forgot to do Sam's. I must remember in the morning. I look at my face in the mirror. I look like my mother.

The TV room is full of white light coming through the thin curtains from the street lights. Samsam is rolled on to her back and has one arm thrown out of her sleeping bag, her fingers curled. I can see well enough to undress and roll out the sleeping bag on the sofa. I can only fit by lying half curled with my knees off the edge. The inner lining is bobbly and smells slightly of wee.

Everything looks pale and shadowy, like a film. Not like my life. There are two little red lights at the bottom of the TV. I imagine they are camera lights. I don't know if I'm in a documentary or a horror movie. I don't know if the audience think I'm a hero or an idiot. I picture Mum and Dad. Dad could drive right past here. He could stop the taxi to check the park. He could pull up right outside. I listen for sounds of cars slowing down. Then I hear the low groan of my phone vibrating. The sound of a text. I lean off the sofa and grabble about on the floor. It's Yas: "Sorry I missed your calls. Phone died. Will call first thing. Think you should come to London."

And now I'm double awake. My charger. I haven't got my charger. I'm trying to remember whether I've seen anyone here with a Samsung. Or a blackberry charger would work. I can only picture iPhones. I text Yas a single "x". Every character uses power, I'm guessing.

So then I lie there. Eyes open. All sorts of questions zoom into my head. What can I do if my phone dies? What if we crash on the way to London? What if I've got this all wrong? I should have spoken to Mum. I haven't even listened to her messages. She might be explaining why the women came. It might not have anything to do with cutting. It uses loads of charge to listen to a voicemail message but I've got to do it. If I write down Yas's number then it won't matter if my phone dies, I can call her from someone else's phone. I need a pen and paper.

I'm out of bed now and searching for my handbag in the white glow. It's at the end of the sofa. There's mints. Crumbs. My purse. My pad. There WAS a pen.

Sam pulls her arm in and rolls on to her side, facing away. I find the pen and write Yas's number on the inside cover of my new pad. I pull my clothes back on and slowly open the door, trying not to make a sound.

I creep to the loo, dial the number for voicemail, and listen: "You have 10 new messages and 8 saved messages. New messages..." Then Mum's voice, shouting: "Answer the phone. For goodness sake, Zahra! What do you think you are playing at? Call us immediately! I'm going out of my mind. How can you do this to Samsam? Right now. Call right now."

It hasn't finished but I click it shut. The green charge sign is down to a thin sliver. I need to talk to her. When she's calmer. When I'm with Yas.

I go through to the kitchen to get a glass of water. Without drawing attention by turning on the lights, I can see well enough to get a glass from the draining board and fill it from the tap.

"Hey."

It's Krysty, sitting on the sofa, in shadow. Which is a bit weird.

"Trouble sleeping?" she drawls, like it's a movie or something.

"Yes."

"Me too. I can never sleep in other people's houses. Especially if I'm nervous."

I can't be bothered to find out why she's nervous, but she's determined to tell me.

"I don't know how this guy Tony is going to react."

"React to what?" I can hear my words speeding up the more she drags hers out.

"To seeing ME." She laughs.

"Isn't he expecting you?"

"No. He's rubbish at keeping in touch, so I thought I'd go and, like, surprise him."

"Really?"

"Yeah, well I don't care anyway if he doesn't want to see me. I can go and stay with my Dad instead if it doesn't work out with Tony."

"OK." I thought it was meant to be a day trip.

"They live very close. They're good mates in fact. Dad was at school in Warsaw with Tony's girlfriend Martyna."

"I'm confused."

"Tony's girlfriend, Martyna, she's Polish too. She knew Dad when they were children and she came to England first so when Dad moved here, he stayed with them. Me and my sister and my Mum came later."

"OK." I'm not really following.

"Martyna and Tony run this café where I used to work."

"But they've broken up?"

"No, no. They're still together, but it's like a convenience thing. He doesn't love her but like there's the café, the kids..."

"They've got kids?"

"Yeah. Two girls: Lily and Ava. I used to babysit them sometimes. Very spoilt."

She pats the sofa beside her. "Don't just stand there looking like a prick at a party, come and sit down."

I do as I'm told. I don't know why. She laughs.

"Don't look so worried. You're worse than me. It's fine. It's all completely secret. Martyna doesn't suspect a thing."

She laughs again. "What about you? What's waking you up in the middle of the night?"

"I don't know."

"That's such a secretive answer! My secret with Tony is like our bond. It's special. We have such a good connection. The problem with Tony is that he lives in the present. He's not good on the phone. You know. Long distance. But when we're together it's great. He's a very generous guy. He gave me these earrings."

She raises up the blonde strands of hair in front of her ears with the backs of her hands. The underneath hair is stuck darkly to her head. She turns her head both ways to show me these glittery silver hearts.

I didn't know what to say. I offer her some water.

"I wouldn't mind a cup of tea."

So we switch on the lights and the pair of us hunt around for the tea things.

"So?" she asks, as soon as she's settled back down with her cup in her hands, "Why are you going to London? Or is that your secret?"

"I'm going to see my friend Yasmin who's at uni there."

"Yes, but why are you here tonight? Why aren't you at home?"

I take a sip of tea. I don't know how to explain.

"I just need to get away for a bit."

"With your little sister?" She looks at me sceptically.

I'm not sure why I tell her. It must be tiredness. I've been lying all day and I've run out of energy for it.

"There are these women I remember from back home. They came to our house this afternoon."

"What women?"

"Women who carry out this practice, of... Well," I pause. I don't know how to sound real. I can't help talking like an information leaflet. "In my culture there is a tradition of, um, performing... of cutting young girls. You know, like circumcision, but for girls. Sometimes it's called FGM."

"Oh my God. What are you saying? That you think that they had come to cut you and your sister?"

"I don't know. I was scared that they would."

"Come on. Surely people don't really do that nowadays?"

"They do. In lots of countries. Egypt, Africa... It's a very old tradition. People thinks it's good, keeps women clean and pure. You know."

She lowers her cup and stares at me. She's got dark panda rings of smudged mascara. "Are you saying they cut off their bits?"

"Yeah."

"Oh my God, that's revolting. Have you had it done to you?"

"No, no."

"So, what, it's like women can't enjoy sex or anything?"

"It's not just cutting, usually they stitch you up... stitch up the vagina. It's so you can't have sex. Not easily. To keep you pure."

Krysty bends forward and puts her cup down on the floor. Then she leans towards me, puts her arms round my neck and pulls me towards her. She smells of Sudocrem. I concentrate on not spilling my tea.

22

MUM DROPPED her shopping and pulled me down: my face was under her arm, my cheek squashed into the grit. Everything had gone quiet. Then a man shouted, and the sound of guns started again.

We lay there for ages until long after all the guns had stopped. She pushed herself up slowly and crouched to lift me. She put her hands under my bottom and I put my arms around her neck. I held on tight with my legs around her middle. She looked around and started a slow run. My bottom bounced on her arms. Over her shoulder I could see the shopping. The plastic bag had split open. The oranges had rolled out on to the road. The bananas were lying there in the gaping bag. Someone was bound to tread on them.

Mum never runs. She is a woman who carries bags or children, a woman whose own body weighs her down. I could hear the air rasping in her chest. She turned a corner and I had a glimpse of the rest of the market. There were stalls and sunshades knocked over, rolls of fabric and suitcases and vegetables spread over the ground. I couldn't see any people and then I realised that everyone was still lying down. I think they were pretending to be dead.

There was suddenly a flash of fire in the sky and an enormous bang. Much louder than the guns. Mum darted into a doorway. For a moment we stood still and then she gently lowered me and held my hand as she pushed at the door. It opened into a hallway. There was a desk facing us, and behind it a chair on its side. On one side there was a wide staircase.

She picked me up again, just on the side of her hip, with my legs dangling in front and behind her and started to run up the stairs. Up to the first floor and round a corner. She was breathing loudly. She put me down again at the top and grabbed my hand and dragged me down this long corridor. She pushed at all the doors we passed. None of them opened, until at last one did and we went in.

There was a table, metal cupboards, a ceiling fan whirring. She dropped down with her back against the door and pulled me in close to her. She put a finger to her lips, and shut her eyes. I leant back against her and felt the rhythm of her chest going up and down, slower and slower.

I don't know how long we were there for. I may even have slept. I opened my eyes and the room was shadowy. It was quiet outside. Mum shifted me off her lap and went to look out of the window.

The corridor was now almost pitch black. We felt our way along the wall towards the dim light of the stairwell. She picked me up again in the hallway. It was dark in the street. Someone on a bike passed suddenly and silently. Just a slight whizz in the air beside us.

We turned into our street. Past the yellow building with the arched windows. Past Bar and Restaurant Dani with its paintings of big plates of rice and curry.

At home Dad was sitting in the dark. The electricity had gone. Mum found a candle and matches and held the light up to his face. He seemed like a ghost. His eyes looked enormous, staring at us, and one cheek was completely swollen. She put the candle down on the floor. It was covered in khat stalks.

"You're addicted to that stuff," she snorted. "I thought you'd be out looking for us."

He spat the green mush into his hand, "What time is it?"

"What time is it? Who cares what time it is? It's night-time. It's dark. Did you even notice we weren't here?"

"What happened?"

"There was shooting in the market. We hid in an office building."

"What office?"

"What office? Why does it matter what office? We hid. We're safe. We're back. I dropped the shopping."

"What?"

She shook her head. "I'm taking Zahra to bed."

She lay down with me and started to sing a soft song to send me to sleep. Her tummy rumbled. I thought about the bananas and whether anyone had trodden on them and whether maybe we'd go back for them in the morning.

23

SOMEONE IS TALKING in a high-pitched American accent. Sam has somehow managed to snuggle on to the sofa beside me. The television is on. There's a grey light through the curtain and possibly the sound of rain. I lean over Sam for my phone. It's dead.

I think through the day. I will borrow a phone and call Yas. I will rub toothpaste on Sam's teeth. We can wash in the downstairs loo and do morning prayers. I can hear people on the stairs and in the kitchen.

"Come on, Sam," I say. "Telly off, clothes on."

"Are we going home?" She asks.

"Prayers and breakfast first," I say. "Let's go and wash."

In the kitchen Lettice is grinding coffee beans. It is raining, but I have to stare hard at the air in the garden to see it.

"Hi girls!" she yells over the din, turning off the grinder and knocking the coffee into a little metal coffee jug. "How did you sleep? Would you like some cereal or some toast? You're first up."

"Pancakes, please!" Sam announces. Mum always makes them and she just thinks it's normal.

"Sam," I whisper, though Lettice can obviously hear me, "Remember to be polite. Have what you are offered."

"Ok, toast."

"Toast please."

Lettice starts cutting bread. "So, what are your plans for today?"

"We're going home," said Samsam.

"Yeah," I hesitate. "After breakfast."

"Oh good. Things more settled at home?"

There's a rumble on the stairs and the kitchen door swings open.

"Why didn't you wake us up?" Annie glares at her mother. "You said you'd wake us!"

"Oh God, did I? I'm sorry," Lettice looks pained.

"Yes – Nick's going to be here in about half an hour and we both need to have showers. It's so annoying, you always say you're going to do something and then you don't."

"I'm sorry," Lettice repeats quietly. "Where are you going?" There's a slight quiver in long thin strands of muscle at the front of her neck.

"Just out," says Annie.

Lettice pushes down hard on the coffee plunger and coffee splurts over the side. She wipes it up and pours herself a cup and takes it with her out to the shed. Studio. The toast pops up.

"He's always late," says Krysty, tipping some cereal into a bowl and sprinkling on extra sugar.

Annie doesn't reply but turns the tap on full blast to refill the kettle.

"Does anyone have a Samsung or Blackberry charger?" I ask.

"We've all got iPhones," says Annie, jamming down the kettle lid.

"Never mind," I say. Which is stupid because I mind like mad. "Would it be possible to have a bit of butter?"

24

WHEN I WAS little I always associated prayers with heels. I could never resist opening my eyes and looking at the upturned feet in front me. The pale pink skin that's hidden from view, until you take off your shoes, kneel in prayer and offer up your tender soles.

25

THERE'S A CAR hooting outside; Annie yells at us to come as she thunders down the stairs. One of the dreadlock guys from the park is standing beside a small battered car and smoking a cigarette. Lettice follows us out and stands for a moment on the garden path; she throws back her head, and offers up her face to the rain. "Feel that softness," she says, "it's heavenly. Let me know when you're going to be back. I'm off to the gym." She turns to me and Sam and hugs us in turn. "Lovely to meet you both," she says and sets off down the street. Rucksack on one shoulder.

Annie opens the car boot and chucks in a bag. "Nick, this is Zahra and Samsam."

"Thanks so much for offering us a lift."

"Not a problem. Always happy to spread the cost of petrol." He grins at me through half-closed lids. I feel sick. I have £15 and I don't know when I'm going to need it.

Annie kicks him, "Don't try it on. You've got your petrol money already. We need to get going."

"Where are we going?" asks Sam.

"I'll explain," I say, "I think we should get in the back."

Sam goes in the middle with Krysty on the far side, glued to her phone. Samsam holds her nose against the smell of old cigarettes. I open the window despite the rain; luckily there's no wind to blow it in. The seat belts have got caught under the back seat and it takes a while to free them. Annie puts on the radio and switches between channels. Nick taps the steering wheel.

I hope I'm doing the right thing. I need to borrow a phone. And I need to explain to Sam what's going on.

As soon as we turn on to the main road we hit the slow Saturday traffic. Pedestrians weaving between the barely moving cars. The rain's stopping. One or two people haven't noticed and are still marching along under umbrellas. I had expected that we'd be out of the city and on to the motorway by now. Any of our neighbours could spot us at this pace. Saturday morning they're likely to be out shopping and Mum's bound to have people searching for us.

I close the window back up and look down at my lap, letting my scarf fall forward over my face. I want to get Sam to lie down without alerting her to the fact that we're hiding. I ask her if she's tired, and she shakes her head. I ask her if she'd like me to tell her a story. I'm hoping she might snuggle down and put her head on my lap. She just wants to know when we'll get home. I say it depends on the traffic. Loud bubbly voices shout from the radio: "Have you been in an accident? You might be entitled to compensation!"

Krysty stops tapping on her phone and for a brief

moment puts it down on her lap.

"Would it be alright for me to make a quick call. I need to phone my friend Yas and my phone's dead."

"Sorry, I haven't got any minutes left." She hesitates, "you can text."

I reach into my bag to get Yas's number. I can't feel the pad. I must have left it in the TV room. I look again, though it's obviously not there. I feel sick. I go through Yas's number in my head and I'm immediately confused. Does it end 3742 or 3472? I try saying both versions in my head. I've lost it.

Krysty passes me her phone.

"What part of London are we going to end up in?"

"Acton. The place is called Polish Café. I can't remember the name of the street. I'll recognise it when we get there. It's left at the big lights."

"Any idea of when we might get there?"

"Never, at this rate," says Nick. I realise he's pulled out his phone and is also texting.

I type "Polish Café. Acton. Not sure what time we'll get there." I send it to the 3742 version and hope for the best.

Samsam leans in to me and whispers, "Why did you say London?"

"These guys have offered us a lift to London and I was thinking it might be nice to go and see Yas." I try to sound light and relaxed.

"Like real London?" she says.

I smile and nod.

"Have you told Mum?"

I nod again: "Why don't you put your head on my lap?"

26

I IMAGINED that as soon as we were on the motorway, I could stop worrying about hiding, but the traffic turns out to be completely stationary and we can easily be seen by other drivers, if not by pedestrians. In fact it's not really hiding that's worrying me. It's whether I've done the right thing. Or why I've done the wrong thing – put us in a car full of people I don't really know or trust – all because of something that might well be a misunderstanding in the first place.

I keep thinking about Mum. I picture her sitting watching telly with Sam on her lap, or in the kitchen in her apron, pots steaming around her. I think of her walking back from the supermarket, weighed down by bags and then dropping down on to a kitchen chair to get her breath back.

Sam sits up and starts drumming her feet on the seat in front.

Annie turns down the radio and looks round to the back, smiling, and asks her to stop.

Sam stills her feet. "I'm thirsty."

"I reckon there's a bottle under one of the seats," Nick shouts.

We all fish about except Krysty who's engrossed in her phone again.

Annie produces a dusty bottle with a millimetre of water in the bottom. I find a pair of scummy socks and two empty beer cans.

Samsam screws up her face.

"Can we get some clean water?" Her voice is whiney.

"We can buy some water when we reach a service station," Annie says with exaggerated calmness.

"I want it now."

"You'll have to wait, Sam, please don't moan."

"How long till we reach a service station?"

"It depends on the traffic."

"I want to get out of the car and go home."

"I know, love, but you can't get out here."

"I want some water. Why are you being so mean?"

"Sam, calm down. We're in a traffic jam. We'll get some water as soon as we can."

"I want Mum." She starts to cry. I'm trying to remember if she did actually eat any of her toast at breakfast.

I try putting my arm round her shoulder but it makes things worse.

"Don't touch me!" she screeches as if I've just physically assaulted her.

Then she starts chanting: "I want Mum. I want Mum."

I clamp my hand over her mouth. I don't know how

else to shut her up. She starts biting at my fingers and wriggles free.

Annie tries, "Hey Sam, look what I've got in my bag."

"I want Mum. I want Mum."

"Come on, love," I say. She gets louder.

Then Nick turns round from the driver's seat and roars:

"SHUT THE FUCK UP!"

Sam's stunned into silence, but he hasn't finished. He's looking at Annie now,

"This is a fucking 'mare. The fucking car's going to overheat unless we get moving. Look at it! It's almost in the fucking red. I don't know why the fuck I said I'd drive you."

Sam drops her head down on to my lap with her hands over her ears. She starts sobbing quietly.

"Shush." I whisper, "Huuwa, huuwa." I try to make my voice as soft as Mum's. And she calms.

We'll come back. That's all I can think. I've been stupid and melodramatic but we can ask Yas to lend us some money and we can get a train or a coach or something. As soon as we see Yas, I'll call Mum and say sorry.

Krysty is holding her phone up to her face and pouting at it. "Hey, Annie," she says, laughing, "Are you going to show Nick those photos we took last night?"

Annie turns round and glares at her.

Slowly we start moving forward and finally reach the roundabout to join the M4. Nick gets in the wrong lane and gets hooted, but at least we're moving. Almost immediately there's a sign to a service station in only 15 miles. The air's strobing through my window so I shut it as Nick speeds up and for a brief moment I feel relieved. We're in the slow lane, but we're moving. Then Nick suddenly pulls into the middle, and then he's swerving back to undertake, then back to the middle, then into the fast. The rain has stopped but the road is shiny, a low grey spray shadowing all the vehicles.

"Hey, stop the zigzag!" Krysty shouts.

"Give over. I'm not an old grandpa. You want to get there, don't you?"

"I'm going to throw up."

Nick doesn't reply. He goes faster.

Then Sam suddenly jolts forward with her hand over her mouth.

"Stop Nick, pull over. Sam's being sick." Annie realises before I do.

We're in the fast lane. We cut in front of a lorry, across to the hard shoulder and slam to a halt. I open the door and Sam leans over me and is sick on to the ground.

"Has anyone got tissues?"

No one has tissues.

"I told you," says Nick.

"I need to get out!" Now it's Krysty fetching up and pulling on her door knob.

"Not the road side!" Annie screams – and we all scrabble out the back, stepping over Sam's sick, so that Krysty can get out. She just makes it to the verge in time and vomits all over the grass.

"Jesus, Nick! You've got to stop at the service

station, and you need to drive more slowly otherwise we're all going to be sick." Annie gets out after us.

I walk along the grass with Sam so she can get some fresh air before getting back in the car. It's raining again, lightly.

We clamber back in after Krysty. Nick's rolling a cigarette.

"This should cover the stench." He strikes a match and has a good suck. He starts the engine.

Annie and I open our windows.

"Has Yas replied?" I ask Krysty.

She shakes her head.

"Can I try a different number?"

"Sure." She passes the phone to me.

"When are you guys planning to go back?" I ask. If I don't find Yas, we're going to need a lift home.

Annie turns around and smiles, "We're going to play it by ear."

Samsam whispers, "I want to go home now."

27

Mum and Grandma and Noor were shaping chapatis, rolling the dough into little balls, singing softly. Grandma always sang when she cooked.

Jim had made a track in the dust. He handed me my marbles. He was going first. He rolled the big marble and then threw three smaller ones at it. They settled in a close circle.

Then it was Yas's go. She always took hers fast. One, two, three. She broke his circle, but each of her marbles shot off so that Jim's were still the closest.

"Your go."

I squatted down beside him and rolled the first, a greeny blue one. It started nicely, heading for the big one, but then it hit an invisible rut and veered off sideways. I chucked the next one and it landed dead, way off. I saved the best till last. I always did. Best in the sense of most beautiful. My favourites were the ones with shimmery surfaces. I tried to skim this last one but it went flying over the top of the lot of them. Useless.

Jim rolled back laughing. Laughing and laughing and laughing at me. His eyes full of tears. His face wrinkled with laughter. Aunty Noor stopped her singing.

"I hope you're being kind to Zahra, Jim!"

I gave him a big stick-out of my tongue.

Yas swept up the marbles, "I'm thirsty!"

We went inside to get a drink. Yas lifted the heavy jug and poured a big mugful of water. She took a swig and then handed it to me. I was just inside the doorway. Outside they'd stopped singing. I could hear my mother sigh.

Aunty Noor was speaking, "You need to face up to it. Look at her. It won't be long. How are you going to protect her? You need to think of the future."

"Anyone can steal from an open purse," said Grandma.

I handed Jim the half-full mug and swung out into the brightness. They stopped talking. Mum stared at the ground. Grandma started singing again. I wished I could understand what I wasn't meant to hear.

28

THE SERVICE STATION car park is absolutely packed.
Nick drives right up to the main building and hangs
around briefly until someone pulls out of a space. Sam
opens the door and slips out.

"Stay there." I don't want her shooting off and getting run over. There are cars reversing in and out of
spaces. Men in shirts are standing beside cars drinking
coffees from big paper cups; women with pale bare legs
beneath summer shorts are lifting kids out of car seats
or digging around in the packed boots of their cars. No
one I know. In fact everyone seems to be white.

"OK. Take my hand and we'll go and find the toilets."
"Anyone fancy a burger?" asks Nick.

No one does. Annie goes to buy water. Sam and
Krysty and me go to the ladies so that they can clean
up.

There is, of course, a massive queue. We stand in
line. The combination of the word toilet and the sight
of the queue makes Sam desperate to go. She's jiggling
around, hopping from leg to leg. The queue shifts
slowly forward.

"I can't wait! I can't wait!"

"Go ahead," the woman in front of us – red rain-coat, tightly belted – shouts up ahead. "This little girl needs to go straight away!"

Hands point us right to the front. No one wants an accident on the floor.

It's only just in time. I go in with her and help her hitch everything up. Then I go after her. I don't want to go right back to the start of the queue, but I feel like I'm taking advantage. Krysty's still queuing.

Anyway, eventually we're out. I rub Sam's face with soap and water and we wash and blast our hands. We go out and into a shop to buy bottled water. Another queue.

"Is this near home?" Sam asks.

"Sort of."

"How long?"

"We're going to go to London first."

"I don't want to go to London." Her voice is rising.

"Samsam," I say, using as calm and soft a voice as possible. "Sam, there's something I need to explain to you."

She looks at me, frowning.

"The ladies who came to our house were bad ladies. I remember them from when I was little. They came to visit when I was your age and they hurt Yasmin, and Rahma... I didn't want them to hurt us. That's why we had to go. We're going to go to Yasmin's in London and we'll stay there till Mum says it's safe to go home."

She looks at me like I'm mad. "How long for?"

"Hang on." We've got to the till. I hand over the £5

note and cup the change in my hand.

"Come and stand here."

I tip the money into my purse and open her water. "We just need to stay out of the way until the coast is clear."

"What coast?"

"Until we know it's safe to go home."

"How did they hurt Yasmin?"

"They cut her."

She wrinkles her nose.

"How?"

"I'm not sure. I just want to make sure we're safe and that they're not going to cut us."

"What if they cut Mum?"

"They won't cut Mum. They don't hurt grown-ups."

I have a horrible thought of Mum as a little girl.

"You should have told Mum you remembered them. She would have pushed them out the door."

"You're right. I should have."

"Is this a made-up story?"

"No."

I suddenly realise that Krysty's hovering. "You guys OK?"

"Yes. We've got water. Have you had a text from Yas?"

"No."

"Can I try another number?"

"I guess."

I try a third combination. The reply is almost instant.

"Text when you get into London."

It's like I've been carrying a concrete bollard, and it's

suddenly turned into a pile of pillows and I'm falling down on top of them.

"What are those orange marks?" says Sam.

"What orange marks?" says Krysty.

"Around your nose."

"Samsam. Don't make personal comments."

Krysty whips out a mirror and starts rubbing her face with two fingers on each cheek. I go to try and find Nick to get an idea of when we might get there.

29

I **WOKE TO** the sound of Mum screeching. There was a weight on top of me and the taste of the city in my mouth. She was calling for Rahma and for a moment I was confused and then I remembered that Rahma was dead. I opened my eyes and closed them quickly against the brown dust. I pushed myself up against the thick air.

I didn't know if I was dead or dreaming.

There was no solid ground. The only clear thing was Mum's high-pitched wail. I tried to find my way towards it. I climbed over rubble, feeling with my hands, scraping my legs. I kept calling but she didn't seem to hear me.

I thought I was choking. I kept stumbling and everything was rough and hard and suddenly there was Mum. Her soft arms. I buried my head against her.

I had no idea where we were. She led the way. She was covered in white dust. Finally we reached some flat ground and could see the whole night sky arching over us.

30

"**O**H, FOR FUCK'S sake!"

I open my eyes. We're in a street of shops. It's hot. I must have slept. I need to text Yas.

"OK, OK. Calm down. Keep going. I know Acton. I'll recognise something soon." Krysty bites her lower lip. You can still see the orange streaks of her foundation.

"I think we should go left at these next lights," says Annie, sliding around a map on her phone.

"What time is it?"

"1.45. What time did you tell your friend?"

"I didn't. I said I'd text her when we got here."

Krysty passes me her phone.

I close my eyes again, and feel the sun through the window. All I can see is my own brownish blood and the imprint of Nick and Annie's head. I remember the date stall in the market. A thousand million glossy sweet dates, laid out above stacks of coloured boxes. Yellow, red, blue.

"Maybe."

"Let's try it, Nick. You go left at the next lights."

Nick drums his fingers in time to the music on the radio.

I can see the date man scooping a heap of dates in his massive hands and dropping them on to the silver scales. He taps my hand, then Rahma's, slipping a sticky date into our palms. "Don't tell your mother!" he jokes.

We turn off the main road and seem to go round in circles. Samsam looks at me with a tired blank expression. Nick's stop-starting and stop-starting and zooming down little side roads. Eventually, eventually, Krysty calls out, "There it is! That's the café!" and Nick jerks the car into a space, and stops.

We're in a wide shopping street outside a launderette. Next door is an "Organic Butcher", all black and shiny, and next to that there's a big pub with tables outside and a man wiping the seats of plastic chairs. The café's on the opposite side of the road. The words POLISH CAFÉ are in big red letters on a white plastic board above the door. There are two men, shaved heads, T shirts, sitting and eating at a table in the window. I can't see a street sign.

"Oh God, that's my Dad. I wasn't expecting him to be here like now," says Krysty. "I can't face this." But Nick's already on the pavement, stretching.

"I think you're going to have to," says Annie and opens her door.

Krysty gets out of the car and adjusts her leggings. One of the men is looking at her. He leans back in his chair and rubs his hands up and down his thighs. They look very alike. Same pointy face. She walks slowly over, shaking out her legs as if they were numb from the journey, and tottering slightly on her heels. He doesn't stand up but opens his arms and Krysty bends down awkwardly to greet him and stands back up quickly. She would have found it easier to balance if she hadn't kept her hands in her pockets.

We all get out of the car. The sky's brightening. Sam clings tightly to my hand and we walk up to the road junction beyond the pub to try and find the street sign so that I can make sure Yas gets the right place. Church Street.

Everyone's gone into the café. Krysty's sitting with her dad; Annie and Nick at another table. Annie's got her hands stretched across the table and is holding Nick's wrist. I hesitate for a moment, not sure whether to join them. There's a woman behind the counter who's staring at us, not smiling. Black hair stretched back tightly, flat against her head. Nick pushes his chair back and Annie pulls back her hands, reaches for her phone, and smiles at us.

"Hi guys! Where did you disappear off to?"

"What do you want?" It's the glary woman; she's come over to Annie's table and is standing into one hip, waiting – pad in hand, chewing gum.

Nick stands up and goes out. He crosses the road and goes into the pub opposite.

"We're not quite ready to order yet," says Annie.

The woman stretches her eyes, "You can't stay if you don't order."

"Sure, won't be a sec. Hey guys, have a look at the menu." Sam and I sit down and Annie passes us a laminated piece of A5.

"Chips, burgers, sausages, baked beans on toast…" the woman lists the options in a monotone.

"Can we have some chips?" said Annie.

"That will be three portions will it? Like I say…"

31

MUM WAS holding my shoulder. We were in the light-house, standing in a kind of hallway. It smelt of the sea, of rotting fish and salt and urine. There was a breeze blowing through. In front of us was a big post, like a stone tree trunk, and around the edge of it a white frill swirling upwards. It was so battered that for a moment I didn't realise that it was a staircase that had lost its steps.

There were voices above.

"Yusuf!" Mum called, and her word echoed.

The voices stopped.

"Yusuf!" she called again, and he appeared, stand-ing at the stop of the staircase, leaning on the central column.

"What's happened?"

"There's been a bomb. I can't find my mother."

"What's happened?"

"I need your help."

He shouted something I couldn't understand over his shoulder and started picking his way down. Slowly. About half way down he dislodged a loose bit of stone and it rolled off the edge, smashing into a small dust cloud on the floor. Someone leant out from the room at the top of the stairs and then disappeared again. Eventually Dad reached the bottom and came towards us unsteadily.

Mum was shaking her head and pulling to go. He put out a hand to me, and covered my hand with his thick warm fingers. I could feel the weight of him as we walked back. Mum pulling ahead, and his hand pulling us down.

32

WE ORDER three portions. Annie pays for all of them.
Krysty is still talking to her dad. Annie lends me her
phone and I text Yas the address. She says it will take
her about two hours.

"Krysty explained what's going on," she says, as I
give it back to her. She looks too keen. I just nod. "Is it
something you've been worried about for a long time?"

"No."

"Did your Mum go through it herself?" She's resting her chin on her hand gazing at me. I can't take the
intensity. I don't want to talk about it. I stand up.

"I'm going to get some ketchup."

Samsam is jiggling her legs and making an eye-
popping, mouth-clenching expression of boredom.

Glary woman slams the chips down on the table,
with a clutch of forks and napkins. One of the forks
bounces off on to the floor. She bends down to pick it
up and her grey white T shirt rides up her back. I can
see a little line of belly hanging over her jeans and the
tight black thong cutting into the flesh of her hips.

I fetch the ketchup from the counter. The chips are a

pathetic effort. Pale and limp, sat in a small pile at the bottom of these fake little yellow plastic baskets. I pick one up and bite into its sagging middle. A mini blast of hot air burns my tongue.

Samsam is blowing exaggeratedly on hers, like Mum has taught her. It's 2.30. I wonder what Mum's doing.

Krysty's dad and his friend are standing in the door-way. They call out goodbye, possibly to the woman behind the counter, possibly to us. Annie replies. He pats Krysty on the back and then he and his friend leave. She drops into a chair beside us.

"Alright?" says Annie. "Help yourself."

I can see glary woman standing behind the counter and watching us.

Krysty shakes her head and stands up again. "I'm going to have a cigarette." She heads out.

Annie's face twitches. "You can finish them," she says, pushing her basket of chips towards Samsam, and follows Krysty out.

There's only me and Samsam left and the woman who is now inspecting her nails. I look at the table, the three baskets of pale chips, and Samsam frowning. I feel like time has gone thick on us, and I don't know how to get back to normal.

33

I COULD HEAR the mumble of Mum and Aunty Noor.
There was no sound of men's voices, so I guessed they
were still looking for Grandma.

My shins and hands were stinging and I had a cut
on my foot that didn't really bother me till we got back
from the lighthouse and then it started really hurting.
Aunty Noor washed it and tied a cloth round it. At first
I tried to lie still so that I didn't disturb Yas and Jim, but
I couldn't sleep. The staircase, the dust, Mum's shriek-
ing. I was going over it all again and again. In the end, I
had to move my arm because it was going prickly with
pins and needles.

"Do you want a story?" said Yas.

And Jim said yes, quick as a flash.

I didn't think he was awake.

"A long long time ago, there was a terrible famine.
The land was dry and bare and the long-eared witch
was roaming the countryside searching for food. She
carried with her an axe and a sack and she searched
everywhere for a delicious girl to eat. She spent a whole
day searching but she found no one for all the people had

110

fled because there was no food. At the end of the day she went home to her daughter, hungry and exhausted. She decided that the next morning she would build a beautiful hut so that if any travellers came through the land they would come to her for shelter and she would be able to capture and eat them.

"So the next day she forced her daughter to build a hut and together they made the most beautiful hut you have ever seen, and sure enough that very night a traveller came knocking. A young widow and her little daughter.

"Now, as luck would have it, the long-eared witch was away fetching water when the pair arrived. They were tired from walking from dawn to dusk, searching for somewhere safe to sleep. The witch's daughter gave them a thin pancake to eat, for that was all she had. She bade them good night and told them not to make a sound. She warned them of her mother, the long-eared witch, and how she loved to eat little children. She promised them that in the morning, at the crack of dawn, before the witch arose, she would come and wake them so that they could go on their way unseen.

"When the long-eared witch came back from the well she immediately spotted that the pancake was missing.

"'Oh, I am so sorry, Mother, I was so hungry I couldn't resist it.'

"The long-eared witch hit her daughter and turned away to stoke the fire.

"'No supper for you tonight,' she snarled. She warmed her pancake on the fire and, as she ate it, she thought she heard a sound.

"'Oh, that is only me Mother, I was humming to myself.'

"The long-eared one finished her pancake and was just about to lie down to sleep when she thought she smelled the flesh of a young girl.

"'Oh Mother,' laughed her daughter. 'It is me you are smelling. When you went to the well I washed in the last of our water. I was so dirty from building the hut.'

"The long-eared witch hit her daughter for wasting the water on washing herself, and then lay down to sleep.

"The long-eared witch snored all night and in the early morning, before the sun rose over the hill the daughter rose silently and went to the newly-made hut. She woke the woman and her daughter and pointed them in the right direction. She was just slipping back into bed when the long-eared witch awoke.

"'Who can I hear running away from here?'

"'No one, Mother,' said the daughter. But the long-eared witch jumped out of bed and saw the widow and her girl running down the hill. She chased after them, shouting back at her daughter, 'Put on a pot of water to boil!'

"So the daughter put some water in a pan and lifted the pan above the fire and stoked the fire, and then she went to see whether the long-eared witch had caught their visitors.

"The woman and her little girl had reached the edge of the valley and there was a deep rift to cross. The woman prayed to Allah to save them and help them over the rift, and suddenly the rift closed and the woman and her child crossed over. After they were safely across, the rift opened behind them.

"Then the long-eared witch reached the edge of the valley, and she prayed to Allah to help her. But Allah replied, 'I only help those who are pure and free from sin.' And the long-eared one gnashed her teeth and pulled her hair but she could not cross the rift.

"She wailed all day but at last, as the sun began to set, she returned home, exhausted and hungry.

"'Lie down, Mother,' said the daughter, 'We have no food but at least you can lie down and rest.'

"So the long-eared witch lay down and she fell into a deep sleep. As soon as she was snoring, her daughter took a ladle. She dipped it in the boiling water. She carried the ladle over to the sleeping witch and very gently, with one hand, she lifted her mother's long ear and she tipped the boiling water right inside it.

"The long-eared witch gave a blood curdling scream, but it was her last. She fell into the sleep that no one can awake from."

34

WE DON'T EAT the chips. I nod a kind of thanks to the woman and we go to join the others. Krysty is standing outside the pub smoking, the others are inside.

It was the first time I've been in a pub. Dark strong beery smell. Nick is at the far end of the room, sitting on a tall stool. He's got a pint of beer in front of him and a big plate of English breakfast. Annie is standing beside him.

"I'm getting a Coke. Do you want anything?"

"We're fine." I don't like how every minute there's a reason to spend money.

The barman is chatting to a customer up the other end of the bar. He looks at us, mutters something and comes across.

The customer starts chuckling. A middle-aged white man. "Glory be!" he goes, loudly. "A burka in a boozer. Don't see that every day!" He bends down to his pint of beer and sucks the thin layer of foam off the top before throwing back his head and laughing.

Of course, neither Sam nor I are wearing a burka, but I guess you can't expect accuracy.

"Can I get you ladies anything?" The barman asks. He's got a smile twitching round his lips. He glances up the bar to the joker, who is still enjoying his own brand of humour.

"Do you serve Muslims? I thought pubs were against their religion."

"Cut it out," says Nick.

Which is surprising.

"No thanks," I say. "We're just looking for our friends. We're going."

We sit down next to Krysty who has sat herself down at one of the outdoor tables and is texting furiously.

The seats are damp. Samsam sits on my lap.

Suddenly Krysty leaps out of her seat and darts out into the road, like a startled deer.

On the opposite pavement there's a bald old man heading towards the café.

Krysty yells something and he stops and gawps at her.

She stops short of him. I can't hear what they're saying. He's got his hands stuffed deep in his pockets and he's jiggling about from side to side. Krysty glances back at the café and then they cross the road towards us.

"Tony, Annie, Nick, Zahra," she nods vaguely in our different directions. She glances at Sam. I guess she hasn't taken in her name.

"Hi guys!" says Tony with a wide smile. He isn't actually bald. He has a rim of blondish hair around the back and sides of his head. And old is unfair. Middle-aged would be more precise. He can't stop fiddling with his hands inside his jogging bottoms.

"Hi," says Annie.

"I gather you're up in town for a bit of fun?"

"Guess we are," Nick pulls on his cigarette and nods his head, smiling like he's got a private joke.

"So, what's the plan?"

There's an awkward silence. Everyone looks at Krysty and Krysty's looking at the ground in this weird stiff way, slanting her head like she's Victoria Beckham.

"Bit of this and that," says Nick.

"Any of you guys smoke?"

Nick holds up his rollie and gives the guy a funny look.

Annie laughs.

"I could get hold of something pretty special if you're interested."

"Sure," Nick's nodding again.

"My flat's round the corner. I'm just going to buy some fags and I'll meet you back there."

Krysty straightens up, "I'll come with you."

"Best not," he says. "I'll see you in ten. You can show them the way, Kryst. Take the keys." He chucks her a bundle, "You know which one it is."

"OK."

He turns to go, but right then the glary woman comes hurtling across the road at the speed of the long-eared witch.

"Martyna, babe! Everything all right?" says Tony. "I was just coming to see if you needed a hand. Looks like things have quietened down though."

"You bitch!" she shouts. She's right up close to

Krysty, spittle in the face. "You bitch! I knew this the minute I saw you. Pretend you come to see your Daddy? I'm not falling for that. You piss off back to the country. I don't want to see you anywhere near my café."

She's jabbing her finger towards Krysty's nose.

"Come on now, Marty." This Tony guy has got his arms round her. "You've got the wrong end of the stick." He steers her back across the road and into the café.

"Let's go," says Krysty.

35

WE FOUND a bone.

We were playing near the rubble. Yas and Jim had
had a row. She wanted to explore. He wanted to play
with a football that he'd found in the street. Yas set off
alone and Jim threw the ball angrily into the air. I stuck
out my hands and it whizzed straight through them, hit
my foot and ricocheted off. I clambered over the ruins
to fetch it.

The bone was long and thin. It was lying on top of
some stones and I didn't see it at first because everything
was the same dusty pale grey colour. I picked it up and
waved it at Jim without really thinking. It was smooth
in my hand. Not heavy. Knobbly at the ends.

Jim climbed up beside me. "It must have been a dog."

"Really?" I put it down quickly. I was scared of dogs.
Their ugly scrawny bodies and their lolling tongues.

"No, a dog that left it here, stupid. It's a man's leg.
But it seems to have been taken away from the rest of
his body."

I started climbing down from the rubble. It's easier
to stop your thoughts when you're moving. I didn't

want to start imagining the person. I didn't want to start thinking about how Jim might know what a man's leg bone looks like.

36

IT'S WEIRD being in this guy Tony's flat without him. Krysty offers us all tea like it's her place, but nobody says yes. Apart from the kitchen and bathroom, there's only one room and a tiny hallway. Nick and Krysty sit themselves on the sofa. Me and Sam and Annie sit on the bed. Krysty points the remote at the telly and we start watching a repeat of Come Dine with Me, waiting for Tony.

Eventually he's there. He plonks 4 cans of Special Brew down on the floor.

"Help yourself."

"Right," says Nick, "cheers."

"So," says Tony, "what's the plan?"

Krysty lowers the volume. "I was wondering, Tony, would it be alright if we stayed the night?"

"Blimey – all of you?" he sniggers.

"No just me and Annie and Nick. You're off, girls, aren't you?"

"Yep," I say.

Samsam pulls my arm and whispers in my ear, "I need the loo."

"Just there," says Krysty, pointing.

"Come with me, Zah," says Sam.

There's a tiny little bathroom with a shower in the bath and a half blackened shower curtain hanging out. The bowl of the loo is stained dark brown. I close the door behind us.

Sam's jaw is wobbling, "I don't like it here." We sit down on the floor and have a hug.

"Please can we go home now? I want to go home and see Mum."

"Ok, OK, don't cry." I hold her tight. "We'll go home. We'll go home as soon as we can. Yas will come soon and we'll make a plan."

37

TONY'S NOW on the bed with Krysty; Annie and Nick are on the sofa. She's sitting sideways with her feet on his thighs. Nick's balancing a magazine on the arm of the sofa to make a little table for his tobacco and he's licking rizla papers and sticking them together. She's laughing like an idiot. I have to get out. Immediately.

"We're going back to the café." I announce. I'm in the doorway between the room and the hallway, blocking it so Samsam can't slip past me. It's not right. She shouldn't be here.

Annie stops laughing and looks at me. "But I thought your friend couldn't get here till 6? Was it?"

"I need some fresh air."

"The café's about to close," says Tony. "You can always come back here."

He smiles at me, and slides his hand into Krysty's shirt.

It starts raining before we get to the café.

Martyna looks up from her phone, "We close at 5. On the dot. No more chips."

"Can I have a cup of tea?" She's never going to let us stay if we don't order anything.

"A woman came, maybe she's looking for you?"

"When?"

"Five minutes? Ten minutes? I tell her maybe you in the pub. I don't know."

"OK. Don't worry about the tea. We'll go see. If she comes back, can you ask her to wait? We'll be back."

"We close in two minutes. If she comes I tell her you in pub."

I think my apprehension must have shown on my face.

"You look in pub. You come back. You wait here. It's better place." She smiles.

She smiles!

The bar man calls out as soon as we go through the door. "There was a woman in a minute ago, looking for you."

"Do you know where she went?"

"Haven't a clue, love, haven't a clue."

"Thanks!" Back out the swinging doors. I look up and down the street. Yas must have got off work early. There's no sign of her. We cross the road back towards the café.

"Who do you think's looking for us?" says Sam. "I hope it's Mum."

I look at her, her tired eyes. I just want to be home.

38

THE DRIVER was standing by the door. Mum waited behind me as I climbed in. Dad was a short way off smoking a cigarette. The bus was hot, airless. It smelt of meat. There were lots of people, bags, baskets. Mum told me to keep going.

"Here," she said, "you go by the window."

The seats were plasticky, unbearably hot. I sat carefully, leaning forward, to keep the sticky heat off my back.

"Oh my goodness!" Mum started fanning herself with her hand.

"Where's Dad going to sit?"

"He can look after himself."

There was a little girl across the aisle staring at us. I turned my back on her and stared out of the window. When the bus's engine started rumbling I had no idea whether Dad had got on the bus or not. Mum's hands were folded on her lap. Her eyes closed. I hoped for the best and looked out over pink dusty hills.

The ride was pretty bumpy. The bus slowed down for bends and then accelerated like crazy on the straight.

I had a horrible low feeling of sickness. I was beginning to feel a bit better after a long straight stretch when suddenly the bus jammed to a halt. The brakes screeched and the view disappeared in clouds of dust. Mum opened her eyes. People were standing up and shouting at the front of the bus. Someone opened the door. The driver shouted back at us in a weary voice: "Road block. Everybody out!"

Mum took my hand. We stayed put and let the queue of people come down the aisle. People were moving very slowly. Women carrying their children. The little girl held her dad's hand. She didn't seem to have a mum. My dad finally emerged from the back and let us in front of him. We were almost the last off. A man in a bright blue shirt was standing by the door, holding a long thin gun. There was a big truck blocking the road. A black flag waving from its roof.

There were about four men with guns and necklaces of bullets getting the passengers into a line. They were wearing army clothes with black and white checked scarves tied tightly around their heads. All you could see of their faces were their huge darting eyes.

The bus driver was talking to the man in the blue shirt. We couldn't hear. One of the soldiers prodded Dad with his gun and pointed him towards the front of the line. We followed him. We had been last and were now first. Dad took my free hand, but he didn't look at me. I copied him and kept my eyes on the ground. The soldiers walked up and down in front of us. They had black boots with laces and khaki trousers tucked in.

"Where are you going?" I looked up. It was the man

in the blue shirt. His head was bare, his scarf around his shoulders. He threw out the words from the back of his throat, jolting his head backwards.

"Kenya," said Dad.

The man crouched down in front of me and looked me in the eyes. His skin was shiny, his face uneven with a deep crease on one cheek. "And you, little girl. Where do you think you are going?"

I felt Mum's hand tightening.

"Kenya."

"Very good." His moustache twitched on the creased side.

He straightened up and moved along to Mum. "Your daughter is pretty."

He put out a hand. Mum hesitated. She reached inside her clothing and brought out some notes. She dropped them into his open hand. She didn't touch him. He didn't move. He waited there, staring at her, his fingers curling down on the edges of the notes, his hand held out, palm upwards, waiting.

She fiddled inside her clothes and brought out three more notes. He nodded; put them in his back pocket and moved on.

Mum dropped to her haunches, and I let go of Dad and crouched beside her.

Then the worst thing happened. I didn't see how it started. Maybe she didn't have any money. He pulled a woman out of the line. She started screaming. I didn't understand. I couldn't see how he was hurting her. He pulled her but she leant her whole weight backwards. So he let go and she stumbled and for a moment she lay there on the ground. He poked at her with his gun. Two of the soldiers came running over and hauled her up. Each one took an arm and they dragged her towards the truck. She kept screaming. When they got to the truck they lifted her, like she weighed nothing, and threw her in the back.

The man in blue gestured with his gun and Dad led the way back to the bus. Suddenly the line was broken and a little boy in a red T shirt started running towards the truck after her. One of the soldiers grabbed him. He picked him up and carried him over to the bus. The boy was kicking against him. Yelling. The soldier put down him on the top step in front of Dad. He ruffled the boy's hair, then turned towards the rest of us in the queue, raising his gun.

It was hard to work out which were our seats because things like the bag Mum left on it had gone. Mum sat by the window this time. She told me to put my head on her lap and lie still. I could hear the little boy crying. When the engine started she let me sit up. I just caught sight of the truck and the man in the blue shirt standing in the back of it waving his gun. My last memory of Somalia.

39

AND THEN she's there. Yas. Yas, with her huge hair bouncing as she looks left and bombs along the pavement towards us; worried and hurried, but right in front of us. I burst into tears.

40

"CALL YOUR Mum." Yas slaps her phone into my hand. I wipe my face on my sleeve. "What?"

"Call your Mum. I promised her I'd get you to do that as soon as I saw you. She's been calling and calling me. So has my Mum. They're in a complete state."

I start to dial. "What shall I say to her?"

"Tell her you're both safe. Tell her you're with me."

The phone doesn't even seem to ring and Mum picks up. She's obviously sitting there, waiting.

I say, "Hi Mum."

Her voice sounds tiny, relieved. "Zahra, oh Zahra. Where are you?"

"We're with Yas. We're fine. I'm so sorry."

She's crying; "Oh sweetheart. Dad will come and get you. He's coming right now. How is Samsam? Is Samsam OK?"

"Yes, she's fine. Have the ladies gone?"

"Of course the ladies have gone." I can hear her irritation immediately. "You think I go on having a tea party when my daughters disappear? Have you any idea how much worry you have given us? Have you any idea?"

"I'm sorry. I'm so sorry. I panicked. I thought they had come to cut us. I was so scared. Because of Rahma."

Mum is silent for a moment. I'm not sure if she's crying. I hear her take a deep breath.

"*In sha' allah*, Zahra. Never question the will of God."

"I know. But I was scared, Mum. I'm still scared. Who are they?"

"You can't blame the ladies for what happened to Rahma. They are good people. Very skilled, very professional. They have a very good reputation."

"Mum?" I feel like my insides are being sucked away. "What do you mean?"

"We're not having an argument. Dad will come and get you."

"Mum. What do you mean? Please Mum. You're not going to get us cut." My jaw is wobbling. I try to hold the air in the top of my mouth. I really don't want to cry.

"You're coming home. You're doing what you're told. Now stop this, Zahra."

"Stop what? Mum, please." I feel like I'm seeping away.

"This running off. This disobedience. You are bringing shame on your family."

"Mum, please." I'm crying and crying. Samsam is holding on to my skirt. Yas takes the phone off me.

130

41

MARTYNA HAS been watching us from the café doorway. She lets me go through to the toilet at the back to wash my face.

Then we go to Tony's flat to tell them we're off. I don't want to but I haven't got their numbers in my head.

Tony comes down to open the door and stands there doing up his belt in front of us. He shouts up the stairs and Annie comes running down. Her cheeks are red. She gives me a big hug. She smells of sweet leaf smoke. "I'm trying to persuade Nick to go back tonight," she said. "Do you want a lift if he agrees?"

"It's fine," says Yas. "They can stay the night with me."

"Are you sure that's a good idea?" I ask her.

She nods a head a little bit manically, "Yeah, think so."

"You could always come with us?"

"I'm fine." She gives us a tight little hand wave. "See you Monday, I guess!"

Yas doesn't want to take us back to her uni halls so

we're going to her friend Patrick's flat. It's two bus rides away, right across the other side of London. We wait for ages on a windy corner. When it finally arrives we go upstairs and sit at the front, three to a double seat with Sam in the middle.

I suddenly feel so tired I can't speak.

Sam pats my arm. "Whisper," she mouths.

I lower my head. She puts her mouth right up against my ear and I can feel her damp tickly breath through my scarf.

"Zah," she goes. "I want to go home."

"I know."

"Please tell Mum."

"Yeah."

"I don't want to go with Nick."

"We won't."

"I'd like to go in a bus or a helicopter or a taxi."

"OK."

42

THE FLAT is on a long tree-lined street with a church at one end of it. There's less traffic here and the bus belts along. We get off at the second stop. Most of the houses have little concrete front gardens with one or two flowerbeds and a row of different coloured bins. Patrick's house stands out because the garden is full of long brown grass and thistles. It's right opposite a zebra crossing. We wait on the pavement, but for a moment it's like we're invisible. In quick succession two cars cross in opposite directions. Yas shouts after them and strides right out. It works: cars stop and we go straight over, through an open gate and into the wild garden and up to a red front door.

Yas bangs loudly on a big metal knocker, and eventually the door is opened by a tall man with a serious smile. We squeeze past a couple of bikes and follow him up a flight of stairs

"You guys can have my room at the top," says Patrick. "It's the biggest. Rob's out tonight, so I can sleep down here."

Yas briefly rubs his shoulder, and takes us up a

narrower flight of stairs which lead to the attic. At the top she pushes open a bedroom door to let us in.

"I'll be with you in a sec.," she says. "Just going to pop to the loo."

It's a big room with a large double bed, a desk and a wardrobe. There's a bookcase which seems to be full of books about science. It's all very tidy. Sam and I sit down on the bed and wait for Yas to come back.

Sam lies back on the bed. I unvelcro her shoes, and kick off my own and lie back with her. We don't say anything. She rolls on to her side and I banana around her, my hands round her tummy.

43

YAS IS SITTING on the floor texting.

"What time is it?"

"Seven thirty."

"Were we asleep a long time?"

"Quarter of an hour? Twenty minutes? Patrick's planning on cooking some pasta. We could go and give him a hand."

The kitchen is small but full of evening light. There's a big view over a car park and a pink sky. The pasta is already on and a pan of tomato sauce is simmering away. Patrick is chopping parsley. He has a big knife and he's holding the handle with one hand and the blade with the other, making tiny fast movements as the leaves turn to dust.

He asks Yas to grate some parmesan and he gives us the job of laying the table.

The four of us squeeze round a tiny table in the corner of the kitchen. Sam carefully removes every miniscule piece of onion from the tomato sauce, but she doesn't complain. The pasta is delicious.

Patrick talks about food. He wants to know what

135

we eat at home, what we love. He's made us a pudding. Strawberry fool. It tastes like heaven. Sam eats every mouthful and licks her spoon clean, which makes Patrick very happy. His face completely crinkles when he laughs.

After supper, Yas says that she and Patrick will wash up if I take Samsam to bed. Patrick lends me his Samsung charger. I take it upstairs and plug in my phone but I don't switch it on. I'll deal with any messages in the morning.

Samsam falls straight to sleep. I lie in bed staring at a line of light on the ceiling. I feel hollow. I can't think what's going to happen now. I think of sitting on Mum's lap and my head fitting into the curve of her shoulder. I think of her voice on the phone, getting colder and louder. The day rushes at me in random pieces: the heat of the sun through the car window as we came into London; Lettice calmly sipping coffee; Martyna with her scraped back hair; the dark sickly sweet smell of the pub; the idiot at the bar and Tony, all flustered and gross in the doorway.

Eventually Yas comes in and opens the window. She climbs over us and slips into the far side of the bed between me and the wall. She lies completely still, but I can tell she's awake.

I whisper, "Yas, are you OK?"

"Yeh." She pauses, "fine. Are you alright?"

"I'm OK. I'm really glad to be here."

"I'm glad you're here." She turns over and faces towards me. "What do you think of Patrick?"

"He seems nice. A really good cook. How do you know him?"

"I met him through a girl on my course. They were at school together."

"So, do you like him?"

"Yeah, I really like him."

"And," I hesitated.

"No." She says, "there's no 'and'. It's complicated."

There's a slight breeze coming through the curtains, wobbling the line of light on the ceiling.

"Yas, can I ask you a question?"

"Sure."

"What happened when your mum took you away from the dancing? I mean in Mogadishu, when the drummers came and we were dancing with Rahma."

"Oh God." She pauses. "Do you remember it?"

I nod. "Yeah. Some things."

She rolls on to her back and she doesn't say anything for ages.

"Do you remember I came over to your house? I was so excited. Jimcaale wasn't allowed to come. Mum said it was a special day for girls and I was like "Yeah, Jimcaale – my special day not yours!" She put on a kiddy voice. Then she was quiet.

"I don't remember where he went.

"Do you remember Rahma spinning round? She was so pleased with her blue dress."

"I remember that. And the three of us held hands and I was so happy because I was in the middle."

We hear a door opening downstairs. Footsteps. I imagine Patrick going to the kitchen, getting a glass of water. We lie in silence until we hear his door close again.

Yas talks in a whisper. "Mum took me home. There were these three ladies sitting outside, waiting." She pauses for a long time.

"I knew something was wrong as soon as I saw them. The house smelt of frankincense. My bed had been pulled out into the middle of the room. Mum told me to lie down..."

Samsam stirs in her sleep and kicks a leg out of the side of the duvet. Yas waits till Sam's breathing settles before continuing.

"I remember Mum holding my chest, pushing me down on to the bed and the women grabbed hold of my legs and I was panicking and screaming and trying to wriggle out of their hands...

"Then Mum shouted at me. She said that I had to lie still or I'd get hurt. And I remember being shocked by the fierceness of her voice and I stopped trying to escape. I lay completely still... That's when they tied a cloth around my mouth. They told me to bite it."

She falls silent. I look at the line of light on the ceiling.

"I wasn't expecting the pain. I hadn't seen a knife or anything. There was just suddenly this screeching pain.

"The next thing I remember is that you were lying beside me on the bed there and I was in agony, needing to pee."

I reach my arms out towards her and pull her close. Her cheeks are wet.

"So I always thought it was my fault. I always

thought that if I hadn't lain still, if I'd gone on fighting, it wouldn't have happened." She wipes her face with the back of her hand. "But maybe that's why it went wrong with Rahma. Maybe she went on fighting."

"I heard her screaming. I don't think they can have managed to gag her."

We lie silently for a few minutes. There are more sounds downstairs of doors and footsteps.

"Does it still hurt?" I whisper it.

"Yes."

I don't know what to say. I stroke her shoulder.

"I'm sorry." I say, "I'm sorry."

"I'm sorry too," she says. She sits up and reaches over me and Sam to grab a roll of loo paper from the bedside table. She tears some off and blows her nose. "I'm sorry," she says again, "but it's not our fault."

44

MUM AND Aunty Noor were standing in the sea. Their long skirts were darkened by the splashing water. I was a long way away up on the beach. I could see their hands flailing as they bent in towards each other. They could have been laughing or crying. I couldn't tell.

45

THE BEDROOM is full of yellow light. The colour of the curtains. Yas's big black hair is spread dramatically all over the pillow.

My head is in a dip between her pillow and Samsam's. I tilt it carefully from side to side to look around without moving my body. I don't want to wake them up. Sam's on her side, turned towards me, breathing softly, smelling of sleep and loveliness. I can see all the tiny little curly hairs which frame her forehead. She looks so perfect and healthy and confident. She looks so like you, Rahma.

I push myself up and shimmy out from under the duvet to go to the bathroom. The door squeaks slightly as I open it. When I get back, Samsam's lying with her eyes open.

"Can we go home today?"

"Possibly," I whisper. "We'll have some breakfast and we'll talk to Yasmin and work out the best thing to do."

"Is Mum angry with us?"

"She's worried about us."

"I want to go home."

"We will. As soon as we know that those ladies are far away and never coming back."

"What do you think we are going to have for breakfast?"

"Cereal," says Yas, pushing herself up and climbing on all fours out of the bed. "I'll just have a shower and then we'll go to the shops. What's your favourite kind? We'll need some milk."

"Coco Pops," says Samsam. "Can we have Coco Pops?"

Yas squats down on the floor and checks her phone. "More calls from your Mum, and a voicemail." She dials up to listen. "She says I must take you home immediately or there will be 'serious consequences'. I'll call her after breakfast."

The stairwell's dark and all the other bedroom doors are closed as we creep down.

Outside it's sunny. The pavement is empty except for occasional runners pounding past. And a short queue of people at the bus stop. We cross the bottom of the road at some lights, a runner waiting beside us, dancing impatiently from foot to foot.

We go into a mini-supermarket and find some Coco Pops and some milk.

"Can I interest you in a bunch of roses today?" The girl on the till asks. She's wearing a headscarf and bright red lipstick. "They're on special offer." There's a bucket of flowers in thin polythene bunches on the counter beside her. "No thanks," says Yas, and pushes her card into the machine. I decide I'll pay for lunch.

Back in the street, a man walks past us with a white pitbull dog wearing a massive studded collar. Yas grabs Sam's arm and swings back around in the direction we've just come from.

"Quick!" She yells. "We'll get the bus."

I think it's because of the dog.

There's a bus at the stop. Yas runs to the open doors at the front, pulling Sam behind her. She flashes her oyster card and scrabbles in her purse to pay for us. We follow her upstairs, lurching as the bus moves off. I still don't know what's going on. It seems mad for such a short distance. We reach the top of the steps as the bus suddenly stops, tipping us again. We're already at the zebra crossing outside Patrick's house. Now I see. There are two men in his front garden. We can only see their backs. One of them is hammering on the door and the other one's hanging behind him. They're both wearing caps. As the bus pulls away, the guy who's hanging back turns around. And as I'm clocking his face he looks up and sees us. It's Mukhtar – what the hell – Uncle Hasan's taxidriver friend. He's shouting something and pushing back the garden gate and tearing up the pavement after the bus. He's young, Mukhtar, and ridiculously tall with bouncy hair that's flying out the sides of his cap. He's fast. I realise the other guy's Ahmed. He's stocky and older and puffing behind. He's never going to catch us, but I'm not so sure about Mukhtar; he's weaving past people, pushing them out the way.

"Shit," says Yas, "Go back down, go back down." The three of us scrabble back down the bus stairs. I'm completely confused.

Yas grabs a hand bar by the exit. "Stand here."

"What are we going to do?"

"If they get on the front of the bus we jump off and run. Otherwise we stay put till we get to the tube station."

"What do they want?"

"I guess they've been sent to take us home? We need to have a proper conversation with your parents. If they don't catch up with us we'll stay on till Elephant and Castle, then we'll get the tube. They'll never find us once we're on the underground. Sam, can I borrow a headscarf?"

"What?" I don't think she's really taken in what's going on.

"They just saw me without a headscarf. If I put on your headscarf, it will be like a disguise."

"But Mum doesn't let me take it off when I'm out of the house."

"Here," I start unwinding my scarf. "Wear this."

I feel naked. Exposed. And my hair's a mess. Yas wraps it around her head, covering most of her face. The other people on the bus are mostly smartly dressed black women in hats and heels and jackets. None of them in headscarves. I'm hoping they don't realise how strange this is.

"Who are you hiding from?" Sam asks.

"Just stupid people. Stupid people. Don't worry. They won't find me."

The bus slows down and a couple of boys come down from upstairs. There are several people waiting at the stop ahead, including a woman with a pram. Two women come forward from the back of the bus and stand beside us. One of them hands me a little booklet and says "God loves you!" in a shaky, enthusiastic voice. The bus stops and all these people push past us as the back door opens. I suddenly realise that this is the door Mukhtar will reach first if he makes it. It's hard to see out of the back window, what with all the smart hats, but I can make him out. He's given up on the pavement and is storming up the road. At the front of the bus the woman with the pram is taking ages, struggling to fold it with her child hitched on to her hip. Meanwhile there's a large woman in peachy satin beside me cautiously lowering herself out of the door. I feel like shoving her. We need this back door to close. Mukhtar is only two trees away. *Close the doors. Close the doors.* I'm panicking that the driver's going to spot him and be kind and wait.

Luckily not. There's a shudder, the doors close and we're off. The pram woman drops into a seat with the child on her lap. There are lights ahead, but they stay green. We swing past them and around a big bend. The traffic's heavy but in front of us is an empty bus lane. I look at the booklet the woman's given me… "What the Bible Really Means". I reach over and drop it onto an empty seat.

46

"RIGHT," says Yas. "Let's go back up and sit down. I'm going to ring this woman Miriam. She's a human rights lawyer and teaches part time on my course. I think she lives in north London somewhere... I'm sure she'll help us if she can."

That's when I realise that my phone is still plugged in to charge in Yas's bedroom.

We find seats on the top deck and Yas pulls out her phone.

"Has Mum called?"

"Loads of times. Eight missed calls. This morning. And my Mum, and your Dad. We'll call them as soon as this calms down."

Sam's gazing out of the window. She turns her head towards me, all serious and puzzled.

"Why are there so many hairdressers?" she asks.

"No idea."

"What's Cash 22?"

"A sort of money shop."

"Shall we go there and buy some money?"

"Not now, we're going to Elephant and Castle."

"Can we play the animal game?"

"Ant," I say.

"Tiger."

"Rat."

And so on until we're at the tube station, and Yas is dragging us towards the ticket machines and the men are nowhere to be seen.

47

EVERYTHING ABOUT Miriam is white – her smiley teeth, the carpet she stands on, the walls behind her, everything except her beautiful brown skin and her silver toenails. She opens the door to her flat, dressed in two towels, both white and fluffy – one wrapped around her body, the other turbaning her head.

"It's lucky you caught me. I was about to leave for work. We've got a big case going to court on Monday. Help yourself to breakfast. I've got to get my shnazzle together. We'll have a proper talk when I get home and you can give me the background. Make yourself at home. There's coffee, milk, juice... croissants, I think, though they're from yesterday. Do use the phone, computer. Whatever you need. The wifi code is on the fridge. The spare keys, in case you need to go out, are on that hook. I'll get something for supper. We can work out bedding later. And girls..." she turns to me, "don't worry. I'm sure we'll be able to get you the support you need. I'll only be a few hours and then we can talk it all through."

Yas gives her a big hug. Then she pulls the Coco

Pops and milk out of her bag. "Come on! We deserve breakfast."

"Have it out on the balcony!" Miriam calls, disappearing down the corridor. "It's a beautiful morning!"

We sit at a little table looking out over grey rooftops. There's an amazing view of a whole hidden world of sky gardens. Every house seems to have some kind of balcony or flat roof for a table and chairs and spikey plants.

After a while Miriam reappears, now dressed in a smart grey suit.

"Bye, girls. I'll see you later. Make yourselves at home."

Yas leaves us out on the balcony and goes inside to call Mum. After a few minutes she brings me the phone, and takes Sam to get the telly working.

Mum's crying. She says she feels ashamed. My heart leaps. But then she explains. She's ashamed of having runaway daughters. What will people think of her if she can't even control her own daughters? I've humiliated her.

I try telling her. We'll come home as soon as we know it's safe. "Please, Mum."

A thin woman in a small summer dress has come out on her roof terrace opposite and is filling a birdfeeder.

Mum's wailing turns to sobbing. She's repeating something through her sobs which I can't understand. Something about Grandma. Dad takes the phone from her: "Why have you brought us this shame? Have you turned against your religion? Why are you doing this Zahra? Why are you humiliating us? You can hear what a state your mother is in."

"I'm sorry. I'm sorry. I don't want to upset anyone. But I don't want to be cut and I don't want Sam to be cut."

"Your mother wants to talk to Sam."

I go inside. Sam's sitting on this big L-shaped sofa with her thumb in her mouth. Mum comes back on the phone, still sobbing.

"She's watching TV. She's fine. I don't want her to get upset." I step back out on the balcony.

"Watching TV? Where are you?"

"It doesn't matter where we are. We are safe. We want to come home. As soon as you promise us..."

At this point Mum screams. "You want ME to promise to YOU? What kind of a daughter are you? Where's your respect? All I want is for you to have a good life. What kind of a future will you have if you don't get a good husband? Your grandmother would be so upset to hear you."

"Mum, can't you listen to me?"

"Why should I listen to you? You should listen to me!"

I start saying something but then I realise no one's there. Dad comes back on the phone; he sounds tired. "Your mother's upset. We'll call back shortly."

Yas is sitting at Miriam's computer. "We need to find someone she will listen to. I'm going to call the mosque."

48

I SAW THE OUTLINE of Dad long before I could see that it was definitely him. I could see the glint of the knife in his hand as the sun hit it. He was leaning forward with a bundle of sticks on his back.

Our old house had been built of stone by my grandfather, but Dad was making our new one out of sticks and cloth. They were ready-made tents in the middle of the refugee camp, but here, on the outskirts, everyone made their own.

Mum looked up as he reached us, but she stayed sitting on the ground.

He scored a circle in the sand. He wanted Mum to check the size. She shrugged. She wiped a hand across her eyes and looked away. There was a low wind.

I helped him separate the sticks by size; he tested each one for bendiness. He laid them out flat and I stood on one end while he pulled the other end into the air. Some of them curled, some of them stayed straight.

He took the biggest ones, the stiffer ones, and stabbed them into the ground along the circle he had marked. Now there was an inside and an outside. I went inside to watch. There was a gap for the door. From inside I watched this man who was watching Dad from the outside, standing with his hands behind his back, looking angry.

Dad took the thinner sticks and bent them over to make a roof. He tied them to the upright sticks and to each other, making a spider's web of bits of old rope and ribbons of cloth and strips of plastic bags. He let me do some of the knotting.

Finally, he stretched cloths over the sticks. I helped him tie them to the sticks. All the cloths were small, like scarves. Each one only covered a couple of joins. There were little gaps everywhere. When we finished, I was in the almost-dark of the inside. I stepped into the doorway. The man had gone.

"This will do for tonight," Dad said. "Tomorrow I will try to find a tarpaulin. Now let's make a fire."

I looked at Mum. She was looking away.

49

YAS HAS LEFT a message for the Imam. She's spoken to Patrick and now she's popped out to get some stuff for lunch. She wouldn't take my money. There's not much in Miriam's fridge: a tub of hummus, our milk bottle and some figs. Plus there's half a packet of pittas, two croissants, which she'd mentioned, and an unopened packet of rye crackers in her bread bin. The cupboards are more promising – lots of beautiful-looking jars of peppers and olives and elegant bottles of oils and vinegars. But nothing that we can actually eat.

Sam's completely zoned out, lying sideways on the sofa. I try watching TV with her. There's some noisy drama about a goat-like alien flying a spaceship. I feel like I'm getting a headache.

I go back out to sit on the balcony. The roof gardens are all deserted. Someone somewhere is drilling.

I decide to go for a nose around. I start in the bathroom. It smells of warm lemon and roses. There's a shower separate to the bath and all the walls are covered in tiny shimmery blue tiles. At first glance there's zero clutter. But the mirrors are actually invisible cupboards which spring open if you tap them. Inside are bottles of perfume, bath oil, face cream, hair conditioners. Tall glass bottles and lots of little pink and gold pots. A long colour-spectrum set of nail polish.

Miriam's bedroom is at the end of the corridor. I open the door slowly, even though I know she's not there. There are two streaks of light crossing the carpet, jagging up and over this huge bed. Otherwise it's dark. I don't like to open the curtains. I peep through one of them. There's no one in the street. No sign of Yas. Or anyone, except after a minute a man comes out from below me, with a baby strapped to his front. I step backwards in case he looks up.

The covers have been thrown down to the bottom of the bed. The towels Miriam was wearing when we arrived are lying, presumably damp, on the floor. I resist the temptation to pick them up and hang them on the warm rail in the bathroom

There's a whole wall of wardrobes. I've never seen so many pairs of shoes and boots. About 50 pairs all set out on special shelves. Dozens of dresses and coats and jackets on hangers. Lots of them in thin plastic covers. Mostly Western. There's one drawer open with a pair of tights hanging out of it, but the rest of the drawers are closed and I'm not going to open them.

I wish I hadn't left my phone. I don't know what to do with myself.

I wander back to the living-room and sit down in front of the computer.

50

I'VE DONE THIS before. Gone to Somalia on Google Earth. The colours are incredible. The land around is green, but Somalia looks like a pink seahorse resting on a blue blue sea. It's the opposite of Bristol. Bristol is grey surrounded by green. Even the coast is rimmed with grey and the sea is, well the sea is a cheery blue, but it somehow looks thin, while the sea around Somalia looks like it's been painted by an excited child with too much clotted paint on their brush. I like that if you put SOM into the google earth search you get offered Somalia and Somerset.

When you zoom into Somalia it looks marbled. I can get close enough in Mogadishu to see the rooftops. But there's no street view in Somalia. You can pick up the little orange pegman and swing him over the sea to Mogadishu but when he gets there he shakes his little body and zips back to base. I can see the streets. And I can see dots of people. It's amazing how few cars there are, compared to Bristol.

I can zoom right in on our house in Bristol. It feels like I'm spying on Mum and Dad. I can take the pegman and drop him down in front of it. I can see the bins in our front garden, and the little low wall. I can see Dad's taxi parked outside. I can even see the reflection of Dad's taxi in our front window.

I guess one day we'll have this for Somalia, once it's safe enough for pegman to visit.

51

"Why was everyone in the market lying down?"

Mum shook her head and put her finger to her lips.

The ceiling fan was whirring and whirring. Everything else was quiet. I listened hard, trying to work out if there was anyone else in the building, but the only other sound was the sound of Mum's breathing and every now and then the sound of gunfire from the street.

I tried to fit my breathing into the pattern of her breathing. There were big gaps. I had to hold my breath and wait wait wait for the next one. I was getting pins and needles in my underneath leg, but she wasn't moving so I tried to stay still. In the end I slid my leg out straight, keeping my eyes on her face so that I would know immediately if I was doing the wrong thing. Her eyes were closed. She opened them to see what I was doing and loosened her grip. Her tummy made an enormous rumble, and she moved her hand to press it. You could always get caught because of a rumble, or a sneeze.

52

DAD GOT A tarpaulin. It took a few days but he found one that someone had discarded. Or maybe they died. It had a couple of holes in it, but they were easily patched.

His knees bent as he carried it, going slightly zigzag under the weight. Mum took one corner, and I took another and we tried to pull it over the roof.

The man had come back. He stood there with his hands behind his back. I was worried that Dad had put the hut in the wrong place. I was worried that the man was holding something behind his back. A gun maybe. I wondered if Dad still had the knife he used to cut the sticks.

We couldn't get the tarpaulin high enough. Dad's side was alright but the side me and Mum were on kept slipping down. Dad shouted at the man to help us.

He came over to me. I didn't notice anything. He stooped towards the edge I was holding and then took it with his teeth and between his elbows. I stood back and watched as he and Dad pulled the cover over the roof. He didn't smile when it was done, but he looked pleased. From then on he was our friend. I asked Mum if he was born without hands, but she said no. Maybe he stole something or maybe he was unlucky. I asked her if she thought he would steal from us. "That would be hard," she said. "We haven't got anything to steal."

"We've got the tarpaulin." I said. She laughed. "That would really test his teeth."

53

I TRY Facebooking Annie to check that they're OK. She replies straight back to me.

Yeah all fine. In car. Left about an hour ago. Nick's driving. Krysty decided to stay behind. What about you? Mum's been on the phone. She had these two weird men visit who were looking for you. She's freaking out.

_____

Do you know who they might be?

_____

I'm guessing they're friends of my uncle.

_____

My Mum's quite worried about you. She was really pissed off with me for staying in London overnight without telling her beforehand. She really wants to talk to you. She's going on about how she's been negligent. Would you be alright with me giving her your number?

_____

Sure in theory but right now I haven't got my phone. I left it in this house we stayed in, and we're not there anymore.

Such an idiot! lol. When d'you reckon you'll be back?

Depends. I'll let you know. Tell your Mum we're OK

54

YAS PUTS the shopping down on the kitchen worktop.
She passes me her phone, "The Imam called. He wants
to speak to you. Can you call him back? It's the last
number."

I look at the list of calls. Below the Imam's number
there are two calls from my Mum, two from Aunty
Noor and one from Jim.

"What did Jim want? He's not on our case, too, is
he?"

"No. He just wanted to check we're all OK. He sent
love."

"Was he nice, the Imam?"

"He was fine. I'm sure he's going to help us. He's
also concerned that you're both OK, and a bit worried
about you running off."

"Is he angry?"

"No. Go on. Call him."

I click the green phone in the call log. My stomach
fizzes.

A low voice answers. "Ah – is this Zahra?"

"Yes."

162

"So, I understand that you've run away from home."

"Yes. I want to go back, but..."

"And you would like me to go and talk to your parents."

"Yes."

"So. I need to understand what it is that has driven you to take this drastic step. You have taken your young sister with you. Is that correct?"

"Yes."

"So. Why don't you start at the beginning and tell me everything that has happened."

"Um..."

"So. How about the day you left home? Tell me what happened that day."

I start with the visit of the ladies. He doesn't interrupt. I can tell from his breathing that he's listening. I tell him about Rahma, Annie, Yas.

"OK, OK," he says, when I finally stop. "This must all be very frightening for you. I am sure your parents only want the best for you, but sometimes people are confused – what is tradition and what is the true teaching of the prophet. The practice of cutting girls is a tradition going back to the times of the Pharoahs, but it is not a teaching of Islam. I will call your parents now to arrange a meeting. And after I have spoken with them I will call you back on this number. Is that alright?"

"Yes."

"Good. We will have you both safely home in no time."

55

MUM DIDN'T speak on the plane. She sat looking at the seat in front of her, shushing me if I asked questions. I was by the window, looking out over the great grey wing of the plane, the little flashing lights. Beyond, I could see a magical world which I never knew existed: golden light shining on bright white clouds.

"Is this heaven?"

She shook her head.

"Is it like heaven?"

She shrugged.

I gazed and then I slept. Suddenly my tummy lurched and we were dropping, down into a thick world of white cloud which got darker grey and then suddenly we were under the clouds and there was green ground, roads, little houses in all sorts of patterns and clusters, tiny shiny cars. I tugged Mum's arm to show her and she tried to lean across, but she had a big bellyful of Samsam (not that we knew it was Samsam then) and she couldn't lean far enough to see.

56

THE FLAT DOOR opens and it's Miriam.

"Hey guys!" She's talking before she's into the room. "I got away earlier than I thought. How you all doing? Enjoying the *Simpsons*?"

I'm not. I go through to the kitchen with Miriam and Yas. Miriam makes a pot of tea. I try to follow their conversation. Child protection. NSPCC. Social Services. The police.

"You're not going to call the police?"

"Don't worry, honey," says Miriam. She produces a packet of chocolate biscuits from her bag.

"We're not going to do anything without discussing it with you. I'm just explaining in theory, the paths we could go down. The first thing is to see how your parents get on with this Imam."

Yas's phone starts singing. She answers it and passes it to me. It's Dad.

"Zahra." He's wheezing badly. "I'm calling from the cab." He pauses for breath between each sentence. "We had a call from an Imam. I've agreed to meet him. Your mother won't go. They spoke on the phone. She's very upset. I'll hear what the man has to say." I can hear the drag of his in-breath. "Then I want you to come home. Tell me the address. I can drive straight on from the mosque… Get you girls home where you belong."

"Call me after you've spoken to the Imam," I say. "And Dad, have you got your puffer?"

But there's no answer because he's gone.

I give Yas the phone back and take Sam a couple of biscuits and some juice. I sit down beside her and she lays her head on my lap. The Simpsons are still yelling at each other.

57

DAD WAS squinting against the sun. He was sitting with his elbows resting on his knees, one hand holding one wrist, the held hand drooping.

I had saved a short stick from the fire and I was drawing in the dust. It was a picture of our tent with Grandma and Rahma sitting in a garden in the sky above. I'd done them both big smiles.

"Dad," I whispered. "Look at my picture."

He raised one eyebrow.

"Look at my picture, Dad. Can you tell who it is?"

He looked across.

"Me and Mum?"

"No Dad, look. This is our tent and this is heaven. Now can you guess?"

He closed his eyes. "Nice picture."

I scrubbed it over with my foot.

Mum was inside the tent lying down.

"Will Grandma see Rahma in heaven?"

"Of course, she'll be looking after her."

"What do people do in heaven?"

"Well, they enjoy all the riches, delicious banquets

and beautiful jewels and trees and rivers."

Sounds boring. "Are there other children there?"

"Of course. All children who die go to heaven."

"When can we see Yas and Jim?"

"Zahra, please stop asking me questions."

58

I WOULD HATE to be in prison. I get so claustrophobic. I'm really fed up with being stuck in Miriam's flat. I want Mum and Dad to call and say everything will be alright. I want to be eating Mum's chicken curry.

Yas and Miriam are making supper in the kitchen. Rice and something. Sam has fallen asleep on my lap. The TV is still on and I can't reach the remote without disturbing her. I wish there was a Sudoku in reach. I love doing Sudoku with Dad.

The sun's clouded over. We're going to eat out on the balcony. I wish time would move.

There's a book in the library at school called *T.I.L.T.* That's what it says on the spine. And on the front it says *Time Is Like Toffee*. I never understood what it meant before. I can't imagine being back at school.

I don't know what we'll do if the Imam doesn't persuade them.

Time was like toffee in the refugee camp. Except not sweet. Just sticky.

59

I BLOW ON Sam's cheek to wake her. We lay the table.
The little roof gardens are filling with people lighting
barbeques and opening bottles of wine. Wafts of the
smell of burning sausages float between the houses.

Yas serves up in the kitchen and we take our plates
outside. Miriam's talking about the law and prosecu-
tions for FGM, and I know I should be listening, but
all I can think about is Dad and the Imam and why no
one's rung.

We're taking the plates in when at last Yas's phone
rings. She doesn't pass it over. She doesn't need to. I
can hear Mum screaming. My first thought is that the
Imam's called the police or something stupid like that.
But it's worse. There's been a fire at the mosque. Dad
and the Imam are in hospital. Yas just keeps saying,
"We're coming. We're coming."

60

THE HOSPITAL'S bright. That's my main sense.

We leave in such a hurry. We literally run for the train, and drop into the nearest seats and then suddenly there's no more rushing to do.

Yas gives Sam her phone to play with and I watch her staring at the screen. The shine has gone from her eyes.

It's dark when we arrive at Bristol Temple Meads and there's a sharp wind pushing along the platform. Yas's fine in her leggings but me and Sam have to lean against it as our skirts blow backwards.

Uncle Hasan is standing beside his taxi in the rank. He opens the doors. He doesn't say anything. Yas sits in the front. He starts the engine and pulls off.

"I don't know what you lot think you've been playing at."

None of us reply, so he carries on, "I'll take you to the hospital. We'll pick up your Mum. Then I'm taking you all back to our house. Don't imagine they'll let you see him at this time of night."

He turns on the radio.

61

IN FACT they do let us see him because he's in a room on his own. There are several machines behind him, and a drip going into one arm. Both arms are stretched out above the blankets and covered in bandages, even his hands. There's a clear plastic mask over his mouth and nose and his wheezing's louder than ever.

Mum's sitting in a chair beside him. She nods when we go in, sucks in her cheeks, swallows. Sam and I stand awkwardly at the end of the bed, Yas behind us. Uncle Hasan's in the doorway.

"A quick minute with the girls, Fadumo; then I'll take you all home." He lets the door shut him out.

There's a nurse sitting in a corner typing on a computer. She smiles and stands up. She's got freckles, like Annie, and wonky teeth.

"You must be his daughters. Come up here and sit beside him. He is very sleepy at the moment; he's had some strong medication but we are going to bring him round gradually so he'll be more awake if you come back in the morning."

I go over to Dad. His eyes are closed. There's

172

nowhere to touch him except his head and a small patch of shoulder. I stroke his hair. It feels like a strange thing to do. Strange to be so close up. His hair usually just looks grey to me, but here in this brightly lit room I can see the little patches of white and grey and black. The pattern of it.

Sam comes beside me and gently touches his head.

Mum pushes up from her seat. "We'll come back in the morning," she says in Somali. Yas translates for the nurse.

"Goodnight, Yusuf," she says, very quietly. She puts her hand lightly on his bandaged hand, and then leads the way out to the corridor where Uncle Hasan is waiting.

62

MUM SITS in the front with Uncle Hasan.

Yas is in between me and Sam.

I wonder whether maybe you could have survived if you'd been in a hospital. I can still remember the lifeless feel of your hand in my hand.

Yas leans forward between the front seats.

"So, what exactly happened? At the mosque... How did the fire start?"

"Not now," Uncle Hasan replies.

Mum doesn't say anything.

63

GRANDMA CAME to collect me from Aunty Noor's house.

"You be a good girl," she said. "Don't upset your mother."

She clasped my hand tightly, squashing the bones of my fingers.

When we got home, Mum was staring into the fire. There was nothing cooking. She looked up and saw me. Then she closed her eyes and started to shake.

"Come on," said Grandma, fiercely. "It has been three days now. Enough of these tears. Allah has written it. Be patient and you will be rewarded. *In sha' allah*."

I go and crouch beside Mum. Your dress, Rahma, is on her lap. I rub it between my fingers. She lifts me up, she wraps me in her arms and in her shawl and I lie sideways against her, like a baby, my head in the hollow of her shoulder, my legs dangling over the edge of her other arm, rocking backwards and forwards, backwards and forwards, the water of her tears falling silently on my face.

64

At breakfast in the morning Aunty Noor makes pancakes. We're hovering round the kitchen drinking tea.

Mum's sitting at the kitchen table, drinking her tea and staring straight ahead.

I go and sit beside her. I want to touch her but she's got a "you-dare" forcefield around her. I try and use a soft voice.

"How did you sleep?"

She raises her eyebrows and tightens her lips as if to say, "Badly of course, what do you expect?" But she doesn't say anything.

"How are you feeling now?" This time she looks at me as if I'm a complete idiot.

"Can you tell us what happened?"

She rubs her eyes. "How would I know? The police don't tell me anything."

Jim's leaning against the kitchen wall. "I don't think the police investigation has finished yet. They're looking at whether it was deliberate, like arson. Or whether maybe it was an accident, electrical fault."

"It's hardly likely to have been an accident." She says it quietly, barely opening her lips.

"What do the doctors say?"

"I have no idea. I can't understand them. Maybe you will get some sense out of them. The Imam is in intensive care."

All the time she has her eyes fixed on her teacup.

"Here, pancakes," says Aunty Noor.

"Not for me," says Mum.

Jim covers his with honey and butter and rolls it into a thick tube. He eats it standing, then grabs his school jacket and his bag.

65

WHEN WE get to the hospital, Dad's room is full of people, doctors. A nurse comes out and asks us if we can wait in the family waiting-room. A doctor will come through to talk to us shortly.

I translate for Mum, and suddenly she's full of questions – fingers outstretched, and her hands jabbing up and down. I tell her the doctor will come and that we have to wait – we have to leave them to do their work. Eventually she drops her arms and I listen to the nurse's explanation of the route to the waiting-room.

There's a young white woman and a toddler in the room. He is picking up leaflets from a table and dropping them on the floor. His mum's sitting with her legs double crossed, giving him occasional glances. Samsam goes straight over to play with him.

His mum goes, "Nathan, Nathan, come and sit on ⸮ lap."

⸮n't take any notice. He's dropping the leaf-
⸮n's putting them back.

⸮s down heavily and closes her eyes.

⸮ I check through the small selection of

178

magazines on a rack. Not really magazines. They are called things like, "Your Rights as a Patient" and "Dermatology Today."

A doctor comes. She's wearing a green top and bottoms. She takes us through to a little side room with a water machine. She wants to know who speaks English and do we need a translator?

The main thing is that Dad is very fragile. The next few days are very important. He has relatively superficial but widespread skin-burns.

She pauses every couple of sentences and me and Yas explain to Mum, who nods, lips clenched.

The main problem is that he's suffered smoke inhalation. His oxygen levels seem to be improving, he should make a good recovery, although there will be some scarring.

"On his face?" Mum asks.

"There probably will be some scarring to the face, but at this stage we're not sure how extensive that will be. A greater concern at this stage is the impact on his lungs. Again it will take a little while to know how extensive any damage is. We're also focusing on pain management."

She tells us we can go in and see him in about 10 minutes. She asks if we have any questions. I ask her if there's any news about the Imam. She smiles slightly and nods. She apologises that she has to follow guidelines about patient confidentiality, but she can tell us that he is in a stable condition in what she calls "the high dependency unit".

After she's gone, Mum pulls her scarf over her eyes.

I brave the forcefield and rub her back. I can feel her shoulders shaking. She doesn't stop me.

"

WHEN WE GO back up, Dad's looking very different from last night. He's propped up on pillows. His eyes were closed when we first went in, but as we say hello he opens them briefly and seems to smile. They have taken away his oxygen mask and given him a little tube with airholes under his nose. He's still got his drip. There's a new nurse sitting at the computer.

He coughs. "Fadumo." His voice is quiet and husky.

Mum leans in. "Yes, love?"

"Are the girls OK?"

"Yes, they're fine. They're here. Look. Come on girls, come closer so Dad can see you."

"You must look after them," he says.

"We'll both look after them," Mum says. She strokes his hair.

Samsam kisses his shoulder.

"We're here, Dad," I whisper, bending down to his ear. "We're alright. We just need you to get better."

"Rahma," he says. "My lovely Rahma. I have missed you so much."

He closes his eyes again. I look at Mum; she's shaking her head.

"You mustn't hurt these girls," he says.

The nurse is still typing away.

"What are you talking about? Of course I won't hurt the girls. This is Zahra, and Samsam."

He raises his eyebrows.

The nurse is staring at her computer screen. I'm surprised she doesn't look round, but of course she won't have understood anything.

Dad starts up again. He sounds panicky. "You must look after her. She is a good girl."

"You're confused." Mum starts to cry. "Tell the nurse he's talking nonsense!" She clamps her hand over her mouth.

I translate.

"It's probably the medication, and he's very tired." The nurse sounds pretty tired herself. "Or it could be an effect of smoke inhalation. Sometimes that happens but it's temporary. Can you tell your mother that it's best for him if everyone keeps calm."

I explain. Mum dabs her eyes with her scarf. Samsam climbs on to her lap.

67

ME AND YAS go off in search of something to eat, leaving Mum and Sam with Dad. Outside in the corridor, a large weary woman is buffing the streaky yellow floor. Yas takes my hand and interweaves her fingers. We walk in step.

On the ground floor we find a tactlessly named café, "The Spice of Life." It does takeaway sandwiches and crisps and stuff so we get some things to take up for the others. It's windowless and busy. Everyone looks stressed. Lots of medics in white coats or green or blue outfits. Most of them eating fast and alone. They are mixed up with ordinary people, presumably relatives of patients, who are mostly huddled around tables, stirring their coffee with plastic sticks or talking on the phone. There's a woman in a short purple coat earwigging a doctor who keeps staring at his bowl of soup and crumbling up his roll. He looks positively grey.

We buy a salad for Mum and sandwiches for everyone else and go to sit outside on a low wall before taking them to the others.

Yas wants to know if I've talked to my Mum at all.

I shake my head.

"Do you feel safe?"

"Yes. Mum's far too concerned about Dad to think about anything else."

"Because I was thinking of going back to London, but I don't want to leave you if you think there's any chance your Mum might be re-arranging for you to be cut."

"It's fine. I'm sure she's not. Not at the moment."

"I just want to go for a few days. I need to get some books at least. I've got exams in a couple of weeks."

"Oh Yas, don't worry. You must go and do your revision and everything."

"I'll pick up your phone from Patrick's"

"Ah, thanks. That would be great."

"Promise you'll get in touch immediately if you've got any worries. Jim has my number."

"I will."

"I want to give you some money, just in case you need to get away quickly. It's only £50, but it could get you and Sam back to London on the coach."

"No."

"Go on. We don't know how quickly things are going to be back to normal. Hopefully there's time for me to do my exams and then we'll sort all this out with your parents. Come on." She stuffs the notes in my bag. "They're going to be wanting their sandwiches."

Back upstairs in the family room, Mum eats a mouthful of pasta salad and then heaves herself up from her chair to throw it in the bin.

Samsam won't sit still and spills apple juice over the floor. I get some green paper towels from the loos but it's hopelessly sticky.

We spend the afternoon in Dad's room. The nurse pulls down the blinds, but it's hot. He sleeps. We sit around. Nobody says anything.

I wonder what people are doing at school.

Mum says she wants to be on her own. So Yas calls her Dad and we go back and wait in the entrance hall for him to come and pick us up.

68

JIM IS BACK from school. Aunty Noor's got her apron on again and she's dishing out some kind of stew. She sits down with us but doesn't eat herself. She puts her feet up on a spare chair. She's only got slippers on but the tops of her feet puff out of them. There's no dent at the bottom of her ankles. Samsam has gone dreamy. She picks out bits of potato to eat.

Uncle Hasan is sitting at the head of the table, tearing up bits of bread and putting them into his mouth at an alarming rate. He stops briefly,

"They think the fire was arson."

"Really?" Yas is gobbling her food. Uncle Hasan is about to take her to the train.

"Apparently the police are questioning some kids."

"Like I've always said," says Aunty Noor. "We're on our own in this country and we have to stick together. You never know what's going to happen."

I take a mouthful of stew, but my throat's closed. I put my hand over my mouth so that it doesn't spill out and I make myself swallow. I can feel tears rising and I don't want that. I stare at the window, the net curtain

186

with the rose pattern that almost reaches the bottom of the window but doesn't quite, the thin line of Uncle Hasan's taxi outside. I swallow and stare and breathe through my mouth till it passes.

We clear up after Yas and Uncle Hasan have gone. Then Aunt Noor walks me and Sam over to our house to pick up some stuff. I notice her limp. She fishes around in her handbag for the key. The bins are full and someone's dog has pooed on the concrete in the front garden.

She bends slowly over as soon as she's opened the door and hands me a paper bag she's picked up from the mat. It's got my name written across it in pink marker pen. Inside there's the notebook which Lettice gave me and a note saying I'd left it on the desk and she'd heard about Dad and was sending best wishes. I'm trying to remember what Annie said about Lettice. Was I meant to ring her?

There's a horrid smell coming from the kitchen. There are big fat flies buzzing around the window. The sink is full of dirty water, and there are used plates and mugs on the side. Aunty Noor was expecting this and has brought her washing up gloves.

Our bedroom has been turned upside down. The mattresses are half off the beds. Our duvets are on the floor. Our drawers are open. We start pushing and folding things into place and I help Samsam find some clean clothes and pack some stuff for myself. We find Lion under Sam's bed. She sits him on top of her pillow. I would have thought she'd want to bring him, but she says she needs him to guard the room so that it doesn't get messed up again. I put the pad from Lettice on my pillow, to sort of match.

When we get back to Aunty Noor's house Uncle Hasan is back from the station but there's no sign of Mum.

"She's going to stay late at the hospital this evening. She needs a bit of peace and quiet, be alone with your father. I've kept some stew for her to eat later."

Aunty Noor starts making cups of tea. Jim goes through to the sitting-room with Samsam to watch the Simpsons.

"You must be tired," Aunty Noor says. "Why don't you go up and have a nice bath? There's some lovely lavender bubblebath you can use. Why don't you get an early night and then you can go in and see your Dad in the morning."

And she's right. I am tired. We go upstairs and she gives me the bubblebath and a big thick blue towel, and says she's going to have a lie down and rest her feet. She goes into her room and switches on the radio. I go into the bathroom, turn on the taps and tip a good dollop of bubblebath into the hot water, before stripping off my clothes and sinking into the warmth.

I lie back, getting wet bubbles all over my hair. I'm thinking about nothing really. The bath gets quite full so I lean forward to turn off the taps, and that's when I hear the cough. From the kitchen directly below me. I stop still and listen hard as the water slurps to still-ness. I can hear the indistinct grumble of noise from the radio. And then again, the low rough cough. It's below me and I know it's the cutter.

I get out of the bath. I unlock the door, grab the towel and wrap it around me as I run past Aunty Noor's bedroom and down the stairs.

Aunty Noor comes straight out after me. She's shouting "Hasan, Hasan. Stop her!" There's no one in the hallway and both the kitchen and living-room doors are closed. I try to open the living-room door, but it won't budge. I can hear the TV from the other side. Aunty Noor comes flapping down the stairs and Jim behind her. The kitchen door is open and I can see Mukhtar and Ahmed standing there.

"What's going on?" I scream. "Let me into the living-room!!"

Jim pushes at the living-room door. Noor's yelling at him to stop. She grabs hold of my towel, but Jim pushes her off me and drags me out the front door.

I don't know what he's doing. He lets go of me and picks up the brick that's holding down the lid of the one of the rubbish bins. He smashes it against the living-room window. There's the sound of glass cracking and he's hitting and hitting it again and again.

I'm standing there in my towel and there's glass all over the garden and Jim's made this massive hole and he's going through it leg first when there's the sound of cars breaking, car doors slamming and then suddenly there's a policeman tugging him back and someone's grabbed hold of me and there's people pushing in through the front door and I don't know what's going on. I keep saying, "My sister's in there, please get my sister!" But nobody's taking any notice of me, and this woman's holding me saying, "Calm down, love, calm down." I'm trying to pull away to get into the house to see if I can see Samsam, but this woman's holding on to me and I'm not going anywhere.

Then a policeman comes out, looks me up and down and says, "You can bring her inside."

We go into the hall. It's crazy. The kitchen and living-room doors are in splinters. We go into the living-room. Samsam's sitting on the sofa with a policewoman beside her. As soon as she sees me she bursts into tears. The policewoman lets go of me and I go over. I'm praying and praying it's not too late.

"Are you OK?" For some reason I whisper it.

She nods. She's still sobbing.

"Did they hurt you?"

"Yes."

I pull her tight. That's when I notice the blood on the floor.

Suddenly the policewoman is shouting. "Have we got an ETA for that ambulance? Can someone get a towel? I need to staunch this blood."

"You'll be alright," I say. I don't think about whether I even mean it. "You'll be alright. I'll come with you in the ambulance."

"Too right, you will," says the policewoman. "Give me that foot." She lifts up my leg and starts wrapping a towel around my foot. "Keep this foot up in the air. You hadn't even noticed it had you? I reckon you're going to need a few stitches."

I hadn't felt it at all. But as soon as I see the cut, all along the side of my foot, I'm hit by a whoosh of sickness and dizziness, and after that I don't remember.

69

I WAKE UP in a strange bedroom. It's full of light. There are two big windows with thin white curtains hanging in front of them, slightly too small. I can feel a dull pulse in my foot. Samsam is sitting cross-legged on the floor, playing with a fat baby doll with a mop of bright blonde hair.

"Are you OK?"

"Yes." She doesn't look up. She's taking the doll through a somersault routine.

"You said last night that the ladies hurt you."

"Yes," she says, sighing. "They were so mean. One of them held my ankles so tightly I'm probably going to get bruises, and the other one pushed down on my chest so I couldn't move."

"But they didn't cut you?"

"No! It was you that got cut. And then we had to go in the amblance." She jumps up and starts running around the room, going "nee-naw nee-naw" holding the doll in the air.

"Come here!" I stick out my arms, "and give me a hug…"

It turns out that we're in the house of a woman called Alison. I'd been given painkillers and was apparently half asleep when we arrived. Alison must have heard Sam playing because she knocks on the door and introduces herself and offers us breakfast and dressing-gowns. Only now do I realise that I'm wearing strange red pyjamas.

I hold onto Alison's soft strong arm and she helps me downstairs. Samsam brings the doll. Apparently I'll be getting a lesson in how to use crutches later on, and I shouldn't be putting weight on my foot. She asks us what we want for breakfast and Sam says pancakes, and she makes them. They're not like Mum's pancakes, but they are quite nice. As we eat, Alison drinks a cup of coffee and tells us about her children. Two boys and a girl. They are grown up now. We can see them smiling at us from silver frames on the walls.

She doesn't know when we'll be going home or seeing Mum and Dad. She explains that a policewoman will be coming to talk to us and we'll know more after that. She suggests I have a bath and stick my leg out of the side. We need to be ready and dressed by 10. I wish I had my phone.

It's the same policewoman as the night before. Tanya. She doesn't look like a policewoman. More like a PE teacher. She walks with a bounce. She's come with someone called Philippa who's a social worker. We go through to Alison's living-room which is cold. Alison pulls back the curtains. It's sunny outside but the sun is going past the windows, not through them. Me and Samsam sink into a big sofa. Tanya and Philippa sit on flowery chairs either side of the fireplace, where there's a display of silver-sprayed pinecones. Alison goes to make coffee.

Tanya does most of the talking and Philippa looks at us through big pink-rimmed glasses and makes notes. Tanya asks about things that don't seem at all relevant. She asks Sam lots of questions about school, the holidays. What language we speak at home. What language we speak with friends. Sam answers in a tiny voice. Tanya smiles encouragingly. She asks me about friends, free time, GCSEs. Philippa looks intently. She pushes her glasses up onto her hair, making it stick out in all directions, lots of different shades of silver and gold. Do we have any questions? Tanya can't tell us when we'll be seeing Mum and Dad either, but she has spoken to the hospital and she's heard that Dad is making good progress and she's sure we'll be seeing him soon. Mum is talking to Tanya's colleagues now, and things will be clearer later.

Tanya explains what's going to happen next. They will need us to go to the police station and they'll ask us some more questions and it will be video-recorded so that we don't have to do it more than once. They just want us to explain what's been going on, what happened last night. She keeps saying that we aren't in trouble and that there is nothing to be afraid of.

Alison comes in with a tray. Coffee, big round white shortbread biscuits, blackcurrant squash. Samsam doesn't want anything. She's let go of the blonde doll which is lying in the crack between the sofa cushions.

She's got dark shiny lines coming down from the inside corners of her eyes. I want Mum.

70

SAM AND I have to do the videoing separately. It's fine. The questions are fine. They don't try and catch you out. They just want it all clear. But I'm worried about Samsam. I don't think she really knows what's been going on.

When we're done Tanya says she's going to take us home. She says Mum's there already.

We sit in the back of the police car and I don't think about what's coming next, just the clean smell of the car and the sunniness outside.

71

MUM ANSWERS the door. She doesn't say anything. I look at her face. I'm dreading the sucked-in, disapproving cheeks and her flat, dull eyes, but her cheeks are soft and I can see the pain in her eyes. I put out a hand and she opens her arms. Sam goes one side and I go the other. We stand there, the three of us, for a very long time. Me with my sore foot in the air.

Tanya says goodbye. Me and Mum go into the kitchen. Sam goes to fetch Lion.

I sit myself down at the table, with my foot up on another chair whilst Mum puts on the kettle. She comes over with the tea and sits beside me. We don't say anything. She sips her tea and looks out of the window. I have to break this.

"Mum," I say quietly. "Had those ladies come to cut us on Friday?"

She nods her head. She still doesn't say anything but tears start falling down her cheeks.

"I'm sorry." She looks up at the corner of the ceiling and tries to swallow her tears. "I am so sorry. I don't know how to explain…"

She wipes her cheeks with quick rough movements of her hands.

"I've always wanted the best for you. Your grandmother... I promised her..."

She keeps pausing to breathe, to hold back the tears.

"I've tried to keep our traditions... Keep discipline, the old ways... What else do we have? Grandma wanted you to have a good life, a good husband. We couldn't help it about Rahma...We tried..."

"I know Mum, I know."

She slaps her hand over her mouth. Her whole body rocks with her sobbing. "I have been such a bad mother." Her words jerk out in spasms. "I killed Rahma."

I'm shaking my head.

"Grandma would be..."

"Mum, come on." I rub her arm. "Grandma didn't know what we know."

She takes my hand and she lets herself cry. Properly. She puts her arms around me. She holds me close and sobs.

In the end, she wipes her face with her scarf and sits back and looks at me. "I always knew. I could remember the pain. And then with your father... I didn't want this for you. But always we were taught that life isn't what you want. You have to be brave, accept the will of God..."

She starts crying again. I suddenly notice that Samsam has come in and is standing in the doorway holding Lion and my new pad. I beckon her to come and sit on my lap.

Mum sees her and fishes a handkerchief from

the depths of her dress.

"I spoke to the Imam on the phone. I talked to the policewoman, the woman from social services…" She strokes Samsam's leg. "I've talked to everybody."

"We should have talked more." I say. "You and me. There is so much we should have talked about."

She nods. "I'm sorry," she says.

I look at her eyes – her soft, dark, water-filled eyes. "It's Rahma… I miss her so much…" She holds out her arms and pulls us both in.

"So do I," I say. "So do I."

72

THAT EVENING Jim and Yas come over. Yas has my phone. They've been talking to the lawyer who thinks that both Uncle Hasan and Aunty Noor will be charged, as well as the cutters, maybe Mukhtar and Ahmed too. Jim and Yas look really tired. Mum makes them pancakes and we all squash round the kitchen table.

"I'm not sure," says Jim, "what's going to happen next."

"What do you mean?" Mum tilts her head.

"I have to go back to London," says Yas. "I've got my exams. I don't know what I'll do but I need to talk to the university."

Mum looks at Jim, "I hope that means you'll move in with us."

He smiles a huge smile and nods and I swear he's welling up, but I can't see because he buries his head in Mum's arms.

"The lawyer did say it was possible that they could get bail," says Yas. "But she said that there's likely to be a condition that they don't have any contact with Sam or Zahra, so they'd have to go somewhere else. They couldn't just go back to living a few doors away, at least until after the court case."

And I suddenly realise what I want to do.

I've realised, Rahma, that all my life I have been talking to you, in my head – and I'm never going to stop doing that. But I never talk *about* you. I want to tell people the story of my beautiful big sister, and why she died. I want everyone to understand why this has to stop. I've got the words, they are all in my head, I just have to get them out...

There on the table is the Indian cloth sketchbook which Lettice gave me. I have already written the opening words:

THE CUTTER CAME LAST NIGHT.

ACKNOWLEDGEMENTS

I would like to offer huge thanks the following people without whom I could not have written this book: Lisa Zimmerman, Hamida Mahammed, Amina Yahaya, Fahma Mohamed, Faiza Abdi, Samia Hachim, Hamdi Muhammed, Hannah Ahmed, Falis Aweys, Fadumo Abukar, Najmo Mahdi, Nimco Ali, Magda Kowalik-Malcolm, Leanne Pook, Jackie Mathers, the NSPCC, Celia Bradshaw, Aurea Carpenter, Rebecca Nicolson, Maud Craigie, Myfanwy Craigie and David Craigie. I would also like to thank Alice Mayers and Joel Wolchover, Maya Kaye, Chloe Lasher, Josie Mayers, Mia Jacobs and Miranda Jacobs. The story evolved from an idea by Anna Baring. *Time is like Toffee* is by Robert Hobhouse.

This book is a work of fiction. The story is placed in a particular time and place but the practice of female genital mutilation is found in many parts of the world. According to the World Health Organisation between 100 and 140 million women and girls worldwide are living with the consequences of FGM.

If you are worried a child may be at risk of FGM call the free **NSPCC** 24-hour FGM helpline on **0800 028 3550**. For more information see **Daughters of Eve –** http://www.dofeve.org

Also by Emma Craigie:

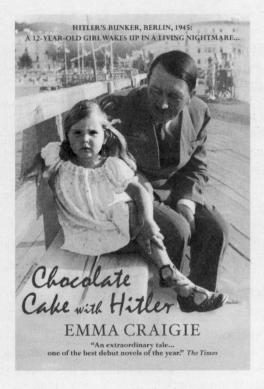

HITLER'S BUNKER, BERLIN, 1945:
A 12-YEAR-OLD GIRL WAKES UP IN A LIVING NIGHTMARE...

Chocolate
Cake with Hitler
EMMA CRAIGIE
"An extraordinary tale...
one of the best debut novels of the year." *The Times*

Chocolate Cake with Hitler is a gripping fictional retelling of the harrowing story of Helga Goebbels, twelve-year-old daughter of the Nazi Party's head of propaganda.

Helga has enjoyed a privileged childhood as the eldest of six children in Germany's First Family, accompanying her parents to parties and rallies, moving between the city and their idyllic country estate.

But the war has changed everything. And now, as defeat closes in on the Germans, Helga must move into a bunker in the heart of Berlin with her family and key members of the crumbling Nazi leadership – to be with their beloved Hitler.

There is chocolate cake for tea every day with "Uncle Leader," but Helga cannot help noticing that all is not well among the grown-ups. When even the soldiers who have been guarding them take their leave, Helga is faced with a terrible truth. Perhaps her perfect childhood has not been all that it seemed...

"An extraordinary and heartbreaking tale that takes you to the dark heart of Nazi Germany."
Andrew Roberts

"Told with child-like innocence, *Chocolate Cake with Hitler* is a poignant insight into the dying days of the Third Reich."
Daily Mail

Maud Craigie

Emma Craigie is a writer and teacher.
She is the author of *Chocolate Cake with
Hitler* and *Who Was... King Henry VIII*
(both published by Short Books). She lives
in Somerset with her husband and four
children.